The Case of the Cryptogram Murders

A Raymond Masters Mystery

Garrison Flint

The Case of the Cryptogram Murders:
A Raymond Masters Mystery, is an original publication of
The Family of Man Press.

The Family of Man Press
A division of G. F. Hutchison Press
310 South Block Avenue, Suite 17
Fayetteville, AR 72701

ISBN: 1-885631-69-3

Printed in USA

PR 10 9 8 7 6 5 4 3 2

CONTENTS

Chapter One
DAY ONE: MONDAY MORNING

The morning was damp. The air, chilled. There was an oppressive heaviness to the low, hovering, gray sky that compacted and exaggerated the unattractiveness of the famous and infamous, old, city. None of this may have been remarkable for late fall in the western suburbs of Chicago but it was not to the liking of Raymond Masters, who despite his well insulated, portly figure, had found himself shivering since entering the cab at the airport hotel twenty minutes earlier. He hoped his hurriedly arranged meeting with Adam Williams would be short, to the point and present an offer that Masters would find easy to refuse. October was his month to vacation in the southwest and the view from the side window confirmed that, indeed, this was *not* New Mexico.

Masters had agreed to the get-together as a favor to a mutual friend who had requested that he speak with Williams about concerns for his personal safety. The old detective had just finished another 'death threat' case in Arkansas* (interrupting another vacation) and found that protecting someone's life was much more demanding than finding the murderer once the deed had taken place. He would not, of course, propose that solution to Mr. Williams.

The cab slowed and turned into a narrow, long cracked, circular drive well hidden from view by a tall, thick, gray stone wall which surrounded the premises. It was a two story mansion – also of gray stone and every bit as foreboding in appearance as the day itself. It seemed haplessly crowded onto a far too narrow lot, but then this was the suburbs and not the wide open spaces of rural western New York where Masters made his home. Another cab was pulling out as his came to a stop at the front door. The rear of a police car protruded from around the far corner of the house.

Masters extricated his bulk from the cab, straightened his coat and tie, (two more reasons he was not happy to be there), brushed his ever wayward mustache into submission, and approached the door. It opened before he could ring the bell.

"Detective Masters, I presume?" the black suited older gentleman said, no genuine question in his tone.

"Yes. Call me Ray, please."

"I'm Raggs. If you will follow me . . . Sir."

The butler's all quite deliberate choice of the word *sir*, effectively side-stepped the issue of familiarity for the moment and the old detective took note. Raggs was the embodiment of a gentleman's gentleman – slender, with flawless erect posture, an English accent, white hair, and a narrow, well groomed, graying mustache, which was the immediate envy of Mr. Masters. He seemed a perfect match to the house but not to the geography. Masters was intrigued.

The lavish, formal, white tiled, entry hall had clearly been designed for entertaining large gatherings and had probably done so many times during its century long reign in that historically fashionable neighborhood. They crossed to the rear left of the room and Raggs paused at the base of a wide, curving, seemingly endless, marble, stairway. Perusing the old detective's ample form the butler suggested, "Perhaps you would prefer the elevator." He extended his arm in its direction.

"The stairs will be fine, thank you" Masters smiled, "That is if you think they will handle my weight."

The man nodded ever so slightly, the hint of a smile

telegraphing a warmhearted, *"Touché, Ray."*

A dozen steps later, Masters began having second thoughts about both the elevator and the third blueberry muffin he had earlier enjoyed at breakfast. Raggs was waiting – somewhat smugly Masters thought – at the top. Mercifully delaying the next leg of the journey, Raggs paused a moment while Masters caught his breath and looked around taking note of the elegant though cheerless, dark, mahogany walls and ornately carved matching woodwork. Raggs then turned and Masters followed, erect and matching him stride for stride. Surprisingly, that felt quite good – it was his turn to feel smug and he flaunted it shamelessly.

"Mr. Williams' study, Sir." Raggs opened one of the double doors and followed Masters inside. There were five others already seated in a semi-circle, occupying five of the six substantial, wooden chairs, upholstered in shiny brown leather, and set with precision in front of a massive, beautifully crafted, matching desk. Above the desk, toward the rear of the room, hung a large, black iron, chandelier, lending a masculine - almost medieval - top-heavy, air to the room. Bookcases behind the desk framed the portrait of a distinguished looking man in his mid-fifties. The desk itself was devoid of clutter, save for the ubiquitous flat desk calendar and the unusual sight of five black phones to the right of the chair. A conference table with chairs sat to the rear left in the room and heavily draped windows graced the right wall. A Berber carpet in variegated, muted earth tones spanned the large room, providing the only splash of color and looking apologetic because of it.

Raggs began the introductions.

"Mrs. Dorothy Williams, Mr. Williams' wife; Alexander Williams, their son; John Haven, Mr. Williams' business partner; Betty Lyon, Mr. Williams' assistant and personal secretary; and Officer Roy Killroy, who is the representative from the local police department."

Masters acknowledged each person with a nod as they were introduced. None had stood or offered their hand. One chair near the center, next to the policeman, was vacant. Raggs indicated the obvious - it was for Masters. He took his seat.

It was eight fifty eight according to the garish, large, brass clock on the wall between the windows. No one spoke. Masters made no attempt to intrude himself into the several quiet minutes that followed. The meeting had been set for nine. Raggs left.

Masters wondered why the others were present but assumed he would soon find out. So far, nothing had been as he had envisioned it.

At eight fifty nine, Adam Williams, pushing the upper limit of middle age and looking immaculate in his dark blue, three piece suit, entered the room and strode to his place behind the desk. He immediately took a seat. It was an earlier edition of his face in the portrait behind him. He looked only at Detective Masters, nodding his recognition in a fleeting glance. Adam had a reputation for punctuality, methodical orderliness, and a rude, abrasive, ruthless, personality (several more good reasons to be elsewhere, Masters thought to himself.)

Adam began:

"You have been asked to be here this morning so you will receive this information simultaneously. I have been receiving death threats – three to date. I have determined who I believe is making them and have asked Detective Masters to accept the job of proving me correct."

That would not be a condition to which Masters would agree, of course. (The sunny warmth of New Mexico seemed suddenly closer!)

Adam took a manila folder from the center desk drawer and placed it in front of him on the desk.

"I am not a likeable man. I have never tried to be. At least four of you have legitimate reasons to want me dead. For many of you, your loyalty has long been dependant upon the checks I sign for you each month. I have never been blind to that. Each of you, along with several others who are not present, would benefit in some important way from my death – some more than others – but it seems that only one of you has the guts to try and do something about it. I do admire that person but it will not keep me from crushing the guilty party like a cockroach beneath my boot."

It had been an unemotional, matter of fact presentation. He stood and handed a white, letter size, envelope across the desk to Masters who accepted it without comment and pocketed it without examination.

It was to be the last act Adam Williams would perform, for at that moment the giant chandelier broke lose from the ceiling and came crashing down upon the man, killing him instantly.

It was a horrifying scene even for those who despised the man. Masters stood and motioned people to stay back. He looked toward the ceiling to determine if it appeared to be in immediate danger of collapsing. That not being the case, he deferred the scene to Officer Killroy who remained seated, frozen to his chair.

Sensing that little help would be forthcoming from Killroy, Masters moved to see if he could find a pulse on Williams. As he suspected there was none. Raggs, having heard the commotion, entered the room, soon followed by the maid, Mildred Mitchell.

Masters caught Raggs' eye, pointed at Killroy and offered a shrug of his shoulders as an open ended question. The shrug was returned with the immediately informative twirling of Raggs index finger directed at his own temple. Masters then mimed a phone to his ear. Raggs understood and left to call the police. Mildred was quick to sit with Mrs. Williams and do what she could to comfort her and Betty.

The son, Alexander – handsome, unkempt, 40ish - approached Masters. With a clear lack of emotion, he asked, "Accident, you think?"

He looked up at the hole in the ceiling, twelve feet above. More than a glance of passive interest, it was thoughtful – studious even.

"Lacking evidence to the contrary, that would be my initial assumption." Masters said. "What's above this room?"

"The attic, I guess. Never had reason to wonder before."

"Where do you gain access to it?"

"I'm not sure. Raggs will know, though. He's been here since Eve fed Adam the apple."

It was clearly a blatant, if somewhat esoteric, derogatory reference to his father.

Alexander – Alex, as he preferred to be called, so of course his father never had – looked younger than his years. With the exception of a short period in an apartment near the *Art Institute*, Alex had lived his entire life there in that house – the *Williams Graystone*, as it was known locally. Adam's father – Alex's grandfather - a successful furrier, had built it in the early nineteen hundreds. It was, therefore, the only home Adam had known as well.

Alex showed artistic promise at an early age and his mother had always encouraged it, contrary to – and perhaps because of - his father's desire for his son to carry on the family business. It gave Alex great pleasure to excel in art – the mere fact silently, but forcefully, defied his father's aspirations for the boy.

Alex and Adam were unlike in virtually every way. Physically, they resembled each other only slightly, a detail Alex delighted in regularly throwing up to his father in most unflattering ways. Conversation between Alex and his father had been sparse, except in rage, since he had been a teenager.

Alex remained close to his mother. She was the one true love of his life. He had never married, although women played an important part in his spectrum of entertainment. Women were vehicles to be enjoyed, much like the expensive cars he owned. Unlike his cars, however, he would never love a woman.

Alex had a studio in an area next to and just East of the study. It was a large, airy, well lit space that reflected his artistic temperament and undisciplined approach to life. He had made a great deal of money in his own right, crafting villages of quaint, miniature buildings which he then had duplicated on a large scale and sold as Christmas decorations. Adam both admired Alex's success and despised him for it. That had never been said but was clear to all who knew the two of them. Apparently, Alex would now be even better off financially.

"Do I need to stick around here or can I go over to my studio?" he asked, looking around and deferring to Masters as the person in charge.

Masters roused Officer Killroy who stood and attempted to muster a take-charge appearance. He had heard the question.

"Well?" Alex repeated, impatiently looking back and forth between the two men.

"I suppose if he stays in the house he can leave, can't he?" Masters said, addressing Killroy, clearly designating the officer as the final authority at the scene.

"Yes. Certainly. Known Al here since he was in diapers. Just stay around, okay?"

With a shrug directed at Masters, Alex rolled his eyes, turned, and left without further comment. He gave no hint that his father's death troubled him in the least.

Masters pursued things with the detective.

"Officer Killroy. It's fortunate you were here. I took the liberty of calling in back up for you while you were sitting there reconnoitering."

"Reconnoitering. Yes, I was reconnoitering. Thank you for jumping in. He's dead I suppose?"

"Yes. Instantly. He took a direct hit to the top of the head."

"Terrible thing. Terrible thing." Killroy repeated shaking his head.

Two uniformed policemen entered the room and made their way toward Killroy.

"What's up?" one of them asked, taking note of Williams' body for the first time. "Ugh! An accident?"

"Looks like an accident to me. Does it look like an accident to you, Mr. Masters?"

"Ray, please."

Killroy preened, restating his question with an increased air of personal importance.

"Does it look like an accident to you, *Ray*?"

The two uniforms looked at each other as if they knew things for sure that the old detective had only begun to suspect. The second raised his eyebrows and asked in an overly deliberate manner, "How shall we precede, Sir?"

The comment had been directed at Killroy but, clearly, it was a response from Masters for which he was hoping.

"I'll bet he'll request the coroner, first and then some help from other detectives to get statements."

"The man's a mind reader, men," Killroy said. "Hop to it, now."

He turned to Masters.

"I hope you're planning to stay on the case. We can use all the help we can get."

"Well if it *were* just an accident as it appears, I'm sure my help won't be needed," Masters answered, wanting very much to just walk away and yet drawn to what he was sure *had* been murder.

"Well, at least help me get some statements – as long as you're here and all."

They moved to where Mrs. Williams sat with Mildred, the maid - her long time companion. Dorothy was an attractive, extremely femine, woman, stately in carriage, probably older than she looked. Her hairdresser, not her genes, was responsible for her jet black hair. Still, it fit well with her more youthful features and smooth, natural complexion.

"I know how hard this must be," Masters began.

"It's only hard because of the sudden horror of the whole thing," Dorothy answered, surprisingly composed and candid.

Masters was puzzled. Dorothy continued.

"I'm glad he's dead. We are all glad he's dead. He was a contemptible human being. I'm just still a bit in shock at the way it happened."

"Are you saying you don't believe it was an accident?"

"Accident? Hardly! Creative? Definitely! Murder? *Undoubtedly!*"

Killroy asked his question. "Who do you suspect, Mrs. Williams?"

"Please call me Dorothy or Dot. For thirty-seven years I've hated being *Mrs. Williams.* . . . Who? I couldn't say. Like Adam said, we all hated him. May I go to my room? I'll be there when you need me."

Killroy nodded and the two women left. Betty Lyons, the secretary approached them. Except for the somewhat masculine cut of the pantsuit she wore she could have passed for Dorothy's younger sister – dark hair cut short, soft features, easy on the make-up. There was an independent air about the way she moved.

"So what now?" she asked, also devoid of the emotions usually accompanying such an event.

Masters had his own question.

"Do you know the contents of that folder on the desk under his body?"

"No. I have no idea. This is the first I knew of the threats. On Thursday Adam instructed me invite – no, direct – the family and staff to be at the meeting. Friday he had me call the police and request that a detective come and sit in on the meeting today. He had me prepare the check for you, Mr. Masters, the one you'll find in the envelope he handed you. I only hope it's large enough to encourage you to stick around and get to the bottom of this."

"You believe it was murder?"

"Of course it was murder!" she said, sounding astonished that anyone might consider an alternative.

"You want his murderer apprehended, then?"

"I could care less about that but I'm in his Will and until all this gets cleared up, I imagine that'll be delayed, and I'm really in need of a long vacation."

There was an awkward silence. Betty continued.

"I suppose that seemed pretty crass, didn't it? He meant

something to me once. Five years ago I was his mistress of the year. He became a tender, vulnerable, human being in intimate situations. I liked him that way. Maybe I even loved him. But with Adam, its twelve months and you're out. I knew that. I'd handled his affairs for fifteen years. I guess I thought I could mean something to him in ways the others hadn't. I was wrong. He did remember every mistress financially. I'll give him that. The day his Will is read the room will be filled with painted faced women who'll each be wondering why all the others are present. It'll be quite a hoot, really."

"His wife knows about all this?" Masters asked.

"Sure. Poor Dotty. She's the one to be pitied in all this. I don't know why she stuck by him. Never could figure that one. Alex kept trying to get her to leave the man. I overheard them talking about it more than once. Alex offered to support her. Something fairly powerful kept her here. Like I said, I can't figure it."

"And Alex. What kept him here?"

"His mother for one. He wouldn't - couldn't - abandon her to Adam."

"You said for one," Masters said. "That indicates there is something else?"

"Sure. Just having Alex underfoot drove Adam nuts. That was all Alex needed. The quintessential thorn in the ass - pardon my French. No one ever did that better than Alex. Life will never seem as good to him from now on. He lived to hassle his dad. Give him a choice between sex or hassling dad, and he'd take hassle every time."

"You wouldn't consider him a suspect then?"

"Alex? He's a pussycat. He loved playing with Adam like some helpless mouse. It was his favorite sport. But then, I guess even cats get tired of the game and eventually eat the mouse, don't they?"

Masters assumed the question was rhetorical.

"Is there *anyone* who liked Adam Williams?"

"Adam Williams, I suppose. Thinking about it, though, I'm not even sure if that's true."

"Do you have a best guess as to who killed him, assuming it wasn't just an accident?" Masters asked.

"Not a clue. If I were in your shoes, I'd just call it an accident and walk away. It's good riddance. The World is now a better place because Adam Williams is gone. His killer should get a medal, not be hunted down like some criminal."

"Civilized society couldn't survive if we allowed ourselves to succumb to that vigilante mentality, Miss Lyons".

"You're right of course. But his being gone is going to improve so many lives in such short order it'll make your head spin. You'll see! May I go back down to my office, now? It's unnerving to be here with him like that."

Officer Killroy nodded. "Don't leave for the day until you get the okay, though."

Betty nodded, took one last look at Adam, shuddered, and left the room.

"Guess it's my turn," were the first words from their next visitor. "I'm John Haven, Adam's former partner."

He offered his hand to Masters and they shook.

"You mean former in the sense of *now he is dead*?" Masters asked.

"No, I mean former in the sense that at seven o'clock Friday evening he called me from New York City saying I was out - that he was going it alone from now on."

"How could he do that – dismiss you, I mean?"

Mr. Haven rubbed his well tanned bald head and adjusted his thick, gold-rimmed glasses.

"He held 85% of the stock in our arrangement. He could do anything he wanted to."

"What was your position in the business?" Masters asked.

"Officially, Vice President in charge of finances Unofficially, the guy who handled the books and did all the dirty work that Adam didn't want to."

"Dirty work?"

"Disenfranchising dealers. Calling in arrears accounts. Cutting the margins of low volume dealers. Asking for favors in ways others couldn't refuse. Returning all the calls from dissatisfied customers. If it was a crap job, I got to do it."

"And for this you got . . ?"

"Fifteen percent of the net profit and I'm not saying that was peanuts – it was about three quarters of a million dollars last year. I can put up with a lot for seven hundred and fifty thousand a year."

"So the business was doing well," Killroy said, underscoring the obvious.

"*Darn* well. It was growing by leaps and bounds since we added a line of replicated furs that even experts can't easily tell from the real thing – well, at first glance, anyway."

"Replicated furs," Masters repeated. "What an interesting term."

"Of course it means *fake* but the older, often snooty, ladies, who are our bread and butter, find the new term far more acceptable."

"Why did Adam include you in the meeting today, if he had already fired you?"

"I really don't know. Betty called Saturday morning. Maybe he was having second thought about the decision. Probably not, knowing Adam. I assume there was some other reason. Probably to dramatize my own motive for wanting him dead. I have one of the best you're going to find."

"And what might that be?"

"A ten million dollar life insurance policy. I was the beneficiary on his and he on mine. It's common business practice among partners. He said the policy on him would be allowed to run out the last of this month when it came up for renewal. So, you see, if I was going to collect, Adam had to die in a hurry – within the next seven days to be exact."

"Was there an accidental death clause?"

"Double indemnity. I guess you'll discover that eventually. So, you think there's any chance that this might have been an accident? Really?"

"No way of saying at this point," Masters answered.

"Well, one can only hope," John said, a new spring in

his step as he headed toward the door. "I'll be in the sitting room downstairs finishing up some paper work."

"An interesting collection of suspects," Masters said to Killroy.

"Suspects? So you suspect it was murder!"

"We need more data before we can assume anything, Officer."

The crime scene team had arrived, soon followed by the coroner. Pictures were taken. Objects were dusted and prints removed. The body was given a cursory examination, bagged and carried out like so much refuse. Masters addressed the coroner.

"Instantaneous death due to massive cerebral hemorrhaging relating to a blow on the top of the cranium?" he asked.

"Pretty good for an onlooker," she responded.

"Oh, this is not an onlooker, Ma'am. This is Detective Raymond Masters."

She did a second take and nodded as if in delayed recognition.

"Mr. Masters. Of course. What a pleasure."

She extended her hand.

"What force rousted you out of your cozy cabin on the western edge of Rossville, New York?"

"You know things I would not have expected," Masters said, then furrowed his brow and added the question, "Flint's books?"

"Yup. Read 'em all. He doesn't allow you much privacy does he?"

"He only hears what I want him to hear. I still control which stories he's privy to." [I *could* be just a bit put off by comments like that, old man!]

The coroner went on.

"I'm calling accidental death unless you have reason for me to say otherwise."

"We've found nothing to question that, other than a half dozen suspects who all admit they would have happily done him in, given half a chance."

"I'll add, *'pending further investigation,'* then, okay?"

"Sounds like a safer call, I'd say," Masters agreed.

"Well, we're all done here. You two can get after it, I guess," she said, looking around the room one last time.

"Thanks for your help. If your further examination of the body reveals anything even slightly suspicious, you'll let us know right away," Masters added.

"Sure will. Accident or murder, I'm pretty sure *my* findings will be the same – dead from a bump on the head. Good hunting."

She left. Raggs stood at the door, hesitating, as if requesting permission to enter.

"Come in. Do you need something?" Killroy asked, more brusquely than Masters felt was appropriate considering the circumstances.

"I just wondered if there were something I could do. It is such a dreadful thing. Poor Mr. Williams. Shall I begin tidying things up?" Raggs approached the two.

"Not yet," Masters answered, redirecting the conversation from Killroy to himself. "We need to snoop a bit first. Perhaps tomorrow. To your knowledge was there ever a problem with the chandelier? Had it ever come loose before?" Masters asked.

"Not to my knowledge. It was a bummer to clean, however."

"Bummer?" Masters said, smiling at Killroy as if to ask, 'American slang' from this distinguished Englishman?"

"An expression I picked from Master Alex when he was a teenager, I'm afraid."

"Explain what you mean about the chandelier."

"Well, most chandeliers are on a rope or chain and can be let down to clean and change bulbs and then pulled back up into position. This one is – well, *was* – stationary. It couldn't be moved, so I had to climb a ladder. I don't like heights. It was my least favorite task in the house."

"When was the last time you attended to it?" Masters

asked.

"Yesterday evening, I'm afraid. Does that make me a suspect?"

"No suspects because no crime has been established. Did you detect anything odd about it at that time?"

"Well, no I can't say so. It certainly didn't appear to be loose if that's what you mean. It was much easier to service this time, though. I finished in less than an hour."

"Why was that?"

"Well, the carpet cleaners were here. When they come they move all the furniture into the hall. They shampoo the carpet, leave for a few hours while it dries and then come back to replace the furniture. While they were gone, I slipped in with the ladder and took care of the chandelier. With no desk to work around, and remembering not to look down, it was a relatively pleasant task, in fact."

"How often is the rug cleaned?" Masters asked.

"That's an odd thing, Sir. The first week of every third month – four times a year like clockwork. This time, however, it was the fourth week of an off month. Apparently Master Alex is the one who called them – as an emergency, the way it sounded from the workers. Mr. Williams was in New York City for several days. He just arrived back this morning in fact, so I haven't had a chance to speak with him about it yet."

Raggs' voice trailed off as he realized that conversation would never come to pass. He continued.

"There is one other odd thing about it all. The desk. It is out of position. It is too far forward in the room."

"By how much?" Masters asked.

Raggs moved to the east end of the desk, opposite from the fallen chandelier. It usually sits back here. You can just make out the old impressions in the carpet. It's sitting a good eighteen inches forward of that spot today."

He looked up.

"Why, if it had been back where it belonged, Mr. Williams might not have even been hit."

The two detectives looked at one another. It began feeling more and more like murder.

"We need to take a look up in the attic – to ascertain what went wrong with the device that held the chandelier in place. Where can we gain access?"

"There is a set of pull down stairs in Guy's room. Guy Lester. He's the handyman. His room is just on the other side of this wall, actually – to the west. Follow me and I'll show you, if you want."

"Later, I think. But thanks for your help. By the way, how are you handling all of this?'

"Not very well, Sir. I know most people hated Mr. Williams but he was always fair with me and treated me quite well. Master Alex used to say I was the only one in the house he didn't rant and rave at. I suppose that was true. I don't have an explanation for it. *Oddly*, I was fond of the man and I don't mind admitting it."

"Well, thanks again for your help and I am sorry about your loss," Masters said.

Raggs nodded, turned and left the room. Masters thought the use of the term '*oddly*' had been strange and tucked it away for future consideration.

Killroy had it solved.

"Raggs is the only one without a clear motive. He did it. It's always the butler, right."

Masters smiled and came close to offering a chuckle before realizing the Officer was serious. 'Another bumble headed cop.' He thought to himself. 'Why, oh why, do I get stuck with bumble headed cops??

Masters moved to the desk and the blood soaked manila folder. "Gloves?" he asked Killroy.

"Oh, yes. Gloves. Never leave home with out them."

As he chuckled at his little joke, he took a pair from his inside jacket pocket and handed them to Masters.

"Not allergic to latex are you? Once had a sergeant who was. Broke out into seven shades of red blotches every time he had to wear them."

Surprising to Masters, his large hands slipped into them

with relative ease – not the usual case. He looked at Killroy's hands. They were massive – a mismatch to his short, slender, small boned frame. Masters opened the folder. Inside was a single sheet of paper on which a sequence of numbers had been hand printed. He removed the sheet and took it to where Killroy was standing near a window.

"What do you make of this?" Masters asked, trying to include the man but not expecting a useful response.

"Looks like some secret code."

Again, Killroy was able to confirm the obvious.

"Do you have a cryptographer on staff?" Masters asked.

He received a blank take.

"A code breaker. Do you have a code guy on staff in your department?"

"Don't think so. Can't remember ever needing one before. We'll find one though. You can count on that. We got resources coming out our ears around here. A dozen colleges and universities within easy spittin' distance. I graduated from one myself a few years back."

The conversation was diverting from the business at hand. Killroy took a business card from his shirt pocket and handed it to Masters.

"Detective K. Roy Killroy, A.S.S."

The quivering of his huge belly signaled Master's silent, spontaneous, chuckle. It was, he thought, perhaps the most appropriate degree designation he had ever seen. Still, he had to ask in as serious a tone as he could muster.

"A.S.S. Not a degree I'm familiar with."

"Associate degree in Social Science." Killroy announced proudly. "My major was Law Enforcement, of course. My minor was sociology. It took six years but it's something I'm really proud of."

Masters could see how important it was as well it should be – six years to finish a two year degree was an *unusual* accomplishment by anybody's standards.

"You a college man?" he asked Masters.

"MS from *Harvard*."

"Well, we can't all be *Wilson Tech* grads, I suppose."

Bumble head or not, Masters was coming to enjoy his new associate.

"We do need to get this coded sheet to some experts, I suppose," Masters said, trying to steer the conversation back to the case.

"I'm sure we can make copies for us to study down in the office," Killroy said. "It's on the first floor directly beneath this room, I believe. I was here several months ago on a burglary."

The disadvantages of a mansion – the distance from floor to floor, for one - were rapidly becoming obvious to Masters. Once in the hall, he sought out and used the elevator.

Miss Lyons – Betty - was busying herself at her desk. She looked up as the men entered through the open door.

"Sorry to bother you, but can we make four copies of this sheet?" Masters asked.

"Certainly. No bother. Over here."

She got up and went to an impressive looking copy machine. She reached out for the paper.

"I will need to place it on the machine," Masters explained, holding up his gloved hand. Fingerprints and such, you understand."

"From the folder?" She asked.

"Correct. Ever see it before?" He held it up by its corners so she could look at it.

"No. Looks like some kind of code. That *is* Mr. Williams printing if that helps any. He often printed. His handwriting was beautiful but not necessarily easily read if you understand the difference."

"Yes, I think I do. What about the paper?"

"It's from the phone message pad on his desk. That's a bit strange, actually. For some reason he chose to write this on the back of the message sheet. He almost always used Marquee Watermarked cotton bond. It was overkill if you ask me but then I just work here – or did. "

"Yes, well, I assume Dorothy and Alex will be working

all that out. If you're like most secretaries I've known, you're the only one who really knows how to run the business anyway. I'm sure your immediate future will be secure."

The copies were made and the original placed into a letter sized plastic bag, which Killroy procured from his inside jacket pocket. It seemed to provide an endless supply of a policeman's necessities.

In the hall they met two plain clothes detectives who had finished taking the official statements. Killroy handed the sheet to them and requested they find a 'cartographer' to look at it. They rolled their eyes in Masters direction and took their leave.

The maid appeared and asked them if they'd like coffee or tea. Killroy begged off, saying he had another appointment but that he'd be back shortly after noon. It was up to Masters.

"I would love a cup of coffee. Thank you."

"Sitting room or kitchen?" she asked.

"Sitting rooms are for dreadfully stuffy gatherings. Kitchens are for making friends. The kitchen if you please," Masters said.

Millie – as she preferred to be called – had been with the Williams family for almost forty years.

"Since you were a mere child, then," Masters said at hearing that.

Millie blushed – pleased - but did not comment further. The kitchen was large – long and narrow – with restaurant grey, stainless steel everything. Except for the bright curtains and a variety of cheery wall decorations it would have appeared as austere and dreary as the rest of the house. Millie's nod directed Masters to sit at a small table which sported coat after coat of paint as evidenced by the chips seen here and there. It represented an interesting contrast to the other, relatively lavish furnishings he had seen elsewhere in the house. She brought him a cup and small, candle-heated coffee urn.

It was clear that she had been crying. Masters used it as an opening.

"You were fonder of Mr. Williams than most of the household members I assume."

"Yes, Sir. I suppose that's true. He always treated me kindly – well, between his bouts of yelling - as kind as he had in him. Me and Raggs was both treated very good."

"It sounds like it was better being help around here than family."

"Except for Guy. He's the handyman and he and Mr. W. never got on well. I like Guy. Don't know what it was between them. Never asked. I don't pry."

"I'd rather not drink alone," Masters said. "I suppose there's a cup with your name on it somewhere around here, isn't there?"

"Yes, Sir. Thank you, Sir."

"My name is Ray. I'd rather not be called, Sir. It sends shivers up my spine."

"I'm Millie, but I guess you knew that. I get them same chills when I'm called Mildred."

She shuddered to dramatize the fact and took a seat across the table. You're a detective, Raggs says."

"Yes, I am."

"The death threats?"

"You know about them?'

"I don't pry or snoop but I do listen and watch. In a place like this the help knows things the family don't, you know?"

"Yes, I can imagine. How long had they been going on – the threats?"

"The past two months as far as I know anything about them. They come in the mail – the mailman leaves the mail here – Johnny – I see that he gets coffee and muffins – his wife died ten years ago – he's lonely, you know?"

"I see. But how did you know they contained threats?"

"There was no *contained* to it. They was on the back of oversized postcards. Had Chicago postmarks."

"The threats were just printed there for all the world to see?" Masters asked clearly puzzled.

"Well, yes and no."

"Masters' brow furrowed."

"They were letters cut out of newspaper ads and pasted to the card."

"Still, they were there for the letter carriers and others, like you to read," Masters pressed.

"Well, yes and no."

Masters smiled at her.

"Millie. Can you just explain before I get too old to understand?"

"Well, yes and no. I mean, the letters were all jumbled up – not real words. The notes were written in cryptograms."

"You know about cryptograms."

"I do them from the papers every morning. Mr. W. was a *crypto-nut* just like me. It was something we had in common. I'd get the papers in the morning – he subscribes to three - and copy down the cryptograms – all three carried different ones. Then I'd drop the papers off in the mail box outside his study door. I'd come back down here and begin working on them. We done them in the same order starting with the Sun every day. About ten or fifteen minutes later I'd get the first call."

"The first call?"

"It would be Mr. W. He'd say, 'Well'. If I had the first one figured I'd read it to him. If I didn't I wouldn't say nothing and he would tell me what he found and then hang up. Then we'd start on the second and so on till the third one was finished."

"Sounds like you and Adam Williams had a congenial relationship."

"Yes, like I said."

"Dare I ask which of you was the better at all this?"

"It was a draw I'd say. I had an unfair advantage, of course."

"What was that?"

"Well, if I had good luck on the first one and finished before he called, I could get started on the second. We really didn't have any rules, you know. Once I got that first one on him, the day was usually mine."

"Was he a good loser?"

"Oh, it wasn't winning and losing – really. It was a game between friends, you know."

"Back to the postcards," Masters said. "I assume when you saw the first one you just couldn't resist decoding it?"

"That's exactly right. I thought it was from one of his friends and that I could use it to play a trick on him. When he called with the first answer that morning I was going to read off the message from the card, instead from the paper. It didn't work out that way. I was scared, really scared, after that first one. I never told nobody that I'd decoded it. I just shuffled it in among his other letters and put them in his box."

"Didn't Miss Lyons open his mail for him?"

"Oh no. I took it directly up to his study every morning. He was a stickler about that. He'd go through his personal mail and then send the rest back down to Betty, later on."

"You must have wondered who had sent it – especially after the second and third."

"Of course. I figure it was some business associate he done wrong. Like I said, he was always nice to me and Raggs but I know he was a mean and vicious man when it come to his business. It was like he was two people."

"Do you remember what the notes said?"

"I have copies here in the drawer. I think they was done by a amateur – not a real cryptogram junkie."

"What makes you say that?"

"Well, short ones is real hard because the number of letter possibilities are so few. Longer ones is easier, you see. Well, the first threat had only seven words – usually nearly impossible except – well let me show you. Here. ***P tbb u kbuk Ukud – Syb Dux***. Decoded it reads, *I see a dead Adam –The Man.* Another funny thing about them was that the *I*, the *A* on Adam and the *T* and *M* in 'The Man' was all written in capitals. Cryptograms are always written in *all* capitals. By pure chance, I suspect, the writer chose words that played right into a cryptogrammer's hand. The only two single letter words in the language were both there - the *I* and the *A*. That's always a good starting place. Then the letters *tbb* which became the word *see*. When that form is present - a double letter after a different first one - nine times out of ten it is either the word *see* or *inn* or *too*. Neither *inn* or *too* would fit in such a short phrase so it had to be see. It wouldn't make sense to read '**A** *blank* **I**' at the beginning, so I figured it was **I** *blank* **A**. By then I had the **a**, the **i**, the **s** and the **e**, so I had the ***EA*** in dead. It was a word with the same first and last letter. *Dead* was one of the few choices – *rear* and *seas* the other probables. The most common three letter word ending in ***E*** is *the*. The last word ended in *AN* so again the choices that meant anything sensible like was limited. It could have been *Fan* like an admirer but why would a fan be threatening him. *Man* made the most sense. It couldn't have taken me three minutes."

"My, I am impressed, Miss Millie. There is more behind that apron than meets the eye."

"I'm no dummy if that's what you're getting at. Not educated but not dumb – there's a big difference."

"There is indeed! What about the second card – just the decoded threat not the methodology."

"Number two said, *You will not see another birthday. - The Man.* Two things about the method you *will* be interested in, I think, if you will pardon me. When I figured out that the letter substitutions for the words at the end – '*the man'* – were the same as in the first message, I just substituted what I already had and was half way there. That means it wasn't meant to be hard to crack – just disguised as they went from hand to hand on their way to him."

"Both astute observations, Millie. There is clearly some detective in you."

"The third card used the same substitution pattern and read, *You'll never see the light before the storm – so to speak. The Man."* Like I said I ain't educated but shouldn't that be '*calm* before the storm'?"

"Yes indeed. We would have to ask why the person

made that substitution and if it were intentional or just a misquotation. Knowing what we now know, it would appear that *the storm* probably refers to the falling of the chandelier and that *light* is actually a clue to the method of murder. Not only was it a cryptogram in structure, but its content was a cryptic hint of things to come."

"I hope all this helps some. I'm sure going to miss those morning calls."

Masters nodded and changed the subject

"Tell me about Alex."

Millie seemed relieved. Her face lit up.

"It's like I raised him from a pup. I love him more than life itself. He stops down here every day – sometimes more than once – and he always brings me a flower or a card or some knick knack he's made for me. I got a whole trunk full of things. When he was away at the Art Institute he called me two or three times a week. I think that God gave him a special power to love everybody – well except his father. I've always felt so bad about that. I've tried to talk with him but he brushes it off – says that's nothing for me to worry my sweet head about. I don't know if loving so much can hurt you or not, but I've always been fearful for Alex. Not everybody agrees with me that he's a loving soul, you understand, but that's always how he's seemed to me."

"What about Alex and his mother?"

"Like two peas in a pod. Almost too close if you ask me. They'd do anything for each other."

"Would one help the other kill Adam?"

"Maybe. I really can't see it from either of them, though. They are good folks. I guess even good folks can be driven to do bad things."

"Why did they stick around if they both hated Adam so much?" Masters asked.

"I as much as asked them both, dozens of times. I didn't want to seem like I was pushing for them to leave, you know, but I think they'd a been a lot happier somewhere else."

"But you don't know why they stayed?"

"Can't figure it – Well, Alex probably stayed to see after his mother. But her – I've never been able to figure that."

"Was Adam abusive toward either of them?"

"You mean did he hit on them – physically? No, never. He'd never even paddle Alex when he was a little boy. I don't think he liked to touch him. He yelled a lot at both of them."

"About what?"

"Anything and everything. Alex's grades, deportment, clothes, friends, girlfriends, social life, college, you name it. There was always something wrong with Dotty – hair, clothes, weight, she'd be two minutes late and he'd rave on for an hour. He was jealous of her and other men so she couldn't go out much – he'd accuse her of having affairs, all the time keeping a mistress of his own in that apartment up town – flaunting her, really."

"Dotty knew about his other women?"

"Sure. Right from the beginning. It was like he wanted to be sure she knew about them. Alex found out about them one day when he was fourteen and was beating the beejeebies out of his dad when Raggs and Dotty found them and pulled him off. That's when Dotty started sending Alex to the shrink. He saw Dr. Floyd for a couple of years. I guess it helped because he never attacked his father again as far as I know, and there ain't anything around here that I don't know – except who killed Mr. W. I guess."

"So you're convinced he was killed and that it wasn't just an accident."

"Come now, Mr. M. Me and you both knows it was murder, otherwise you wouldn't be sittin' here pumpin' me and I wouldn't be here spillin' my guts to you."

"Millie, you are quite a lady. How can I thank you for your help?"

"Catch his killer. We owe the man that much."

She stood and wiped her suddenly moist eyes with her apron. "More coffee?" she asked.

"One more time would be great?"

"It's almost mail time. Johnny will be here. We always

used to do the crossword together over coffee. Most days now he don't have time. His route's been lengthened he says."

"I get the idea Johnny is more than just a mailman to you."

"You're a good detective Mr. M. I'm afraid he means more to me than I do to him. I've never been married. Maybe that's part of the difference. The way he's been lately – so standoffish – I suppose I shouldn't hold out no hope about it becoming something."

Masters passed on that one. He removed one of the copies of the coded sheet from his pocket and held it up across the table toward Millie.

"What's your take on something like this?"

She became quite serious.

"It's Mr. W's printing. Is this a clue in the case?"

"I believe it names the person he thinks was threatening him."

Millie continued to look at the page.

"It's no regular cryptogram. In the first place it's numbers for letters not letters for letters. In the second place I don't think its just simple substitution. I'll take a crack at it if you like. I'll just keep it to myself you can count on that. No, this ain't no regular cryptogram. I may not be much help but I'll give it my best shot."

"Okay then, you have just become my number one assistant on the case. I better go before Johnny arrives. I make it a point never to interfere when there is the chance for romance in the air."

Millie giggled and cleared the table. Masters walked back toward the front hall in search of the Sitting Room that Millie had mentioned. He needed a place to be alone. There were far too many suspects. There was far too little evidence. There needed to be a plan of action and for that he needed solitude.

---

* *The Case of the Clairvoyant Kid,* Garrison Flint, 2002, The Family of Man Press, ISBN: 1-885631-58-8

Chapter Two
Day one: Late Morning

The Sitting Room was located just to the right of the staircase from hell, separated from the expansive entry hall by a set of large sliding doors. It was Victorian in style – not at all to Masters' liking but then that was none of his affair. He tried several chairs until he found one that easily handled his figure and promised to provide some degree of comfort for the next several hours.

As he settled in, Raggs appeared next to him.

"A pad and pen, Mr. Masters. Would there be something else you might need?"

"And he reads minds as well," was Masters' greeting as he accepted the material. "Thank you. Most thoughtful. You see, I really had not intended to get involved in this case so came ill prepared, I'm afraid."

"And now you have chosen to become involved?"

"It looks that way."

"May I then send for your things from the hotel? I can set you up quite comfortably in a small suite just down the hall – first floor, I might add. Just a hop, skip and a jump from the kitchen."

There was the twinkle of an Imp in the old man's eye.

It was met in kind from Masters.

"I suppose that would be best although I feel I need to have Dorothy's invitation to enter the case now that Mr. Williams is gone."

"Having you stay here was her suggestion. She asked that I tell you she and the household staff are available to be of assistance in any way. On the phone she is 39. Press the green button on the bottom and then 3-9. I am 6-7 – not my age should you be interested. Miss Lyons is 2-5. May I have your key for the hotel?"

"Yes, certainly. It's one of those confounded plastic cards. I can't get used to this electronic age, Raggs."

"I understand. Not my cup of tea either, so to speak." He smiled an actual, real life smile at what he apparently considered his little joke – so little that Masters had not understood it. Perhaps it was the British sense of humor. Perhaps it was Masters' 'maturing' grey matter. He'd opt for the British thing.

"Raggs," Masters said, merely stating the name. "Would that be a first name, last name or nick name?"

"Last name. Newman Wellington Raggs the Fourth to be completely accurate."

"And is there a Fifth, if I may ask?"

"Yes there is. Attended Oxford. A barrister some twenty years now."

The old gentleman's pride was clear.

"He remains in England then."

"International law. It brings him across the pond frequently. Three grandchildren but not a Sixth among the lot – all beautiful little girls."

It was an openness Masters had not expected but did appreciate. Openness precedes friendship and he felt that he and Raggs could become good friends.

"I'll leave you to your business, then. Ring me when you are ready to see your rooms. Are you coffee or tea?"

"Coffee, usually," Masters replied.

"Me too, but I only admit that to a select few and never

to an Englishman. May I bring an urn?"

"I just exceeded my daily allowance with Millie in the kitchen, but thank you."

Raggs nodded and left as quietly as he had come. Masters settled back and began making notes – a series of questions to be more precise. As he has often been heard to say, "It is the asking of that one right question that proceeds the solving of any problem," and there were several problems associated with this case.

For starters, why had the threats come as cryptograms and on cards rather than in envelopes? They were from someone who knew of his penchant for codes. That could include dozens of acquaintances and everyone in his household. It was as if the taunting of the man had been as important as his killing. But then if taunting were a part of it why make the code so easy – would a difficult message not be more of a threat? Perhaps the killer was, as Millie had suspected, a novice at the cryptogram and not skilled enough to create difficult systems. Or, perhaps it *was* an expert who wanted it to appear to be the work of a novice.

The make-up of that first seven word message made Masters lean toward the latter possibility. It had included those important single letter words "a" and "I" and the tell-tale "see" – all clues that made it easily decoded by a knowledgeable cryptograph fan who would search for them at the outset. Also, there had been only nine different letters used in the entire message, again adding to the ease with which it could be decoded. Coincidence? Perhaps, but Masters was no friend of coincidence and only begrudgingly ever acquiesced to it.

And then, why *three* separate death threats? Most would-be killers found one to be sufficient. In fact, why any threats at all? Why give Adam the opportunity to prepare? There was a game involved. Adam was supposed to squirm. His final days were supposed to be disconcerting. It sounded like revenge – but then murder often was.

Why use letters cut from newspapers? Why not just laser print it from a computer – it would be virtually impossible to trace since each laser pass in a given printer varies from all others. The cut-outs lent a dramatic flair – perhaps more of a challenge to produce – keeping fingerprints clear and so on. There was probably more to it than that. Perhaps the perpetrator was unskilled with computers or even typewriters. That might suggest an older person. Or, it could be the opposite of course, someone all quite competent in the use of printers but who wanted to implicate someone else – someone who was not. Perhaps it was only a ploy to confuse the authorities into thinking it had some significance when in fact it didn't. A final thought on the subject rushed through his mind: Could it have been that they had been sent as cryptograms on open cards knowing that Millie, who received the mail first, would find them irresistible and decode them? But what purpose would that serve? Had Adam sent them to himself in some scheme to implicate someone else, making sure Millie would see them as verification they had arrived through the mail?

The more immediate questions were why Adam chose to write his suspicions about the killer in code and then, how to decode that message.

Masters took out his copy. He carefully read each number group out loud.

4. 5 3 7 8 3 7 2 4 5 5 3 3

4 4 7 6 3 7 4 3 9 ‘7 3 2 8 4 3
7

2 7 9

Several things seemed apparent. If each group represented a word, then there were seven words. There were two strange features – the dot or period after the first number and the apostrophe near the end of the fifth group. Periods usually follow an abbreviation or initial. An apostrophe typically comes before an "s" to indicate possession, or a "t" to indicate a negative contraction. Or, perhaps the dot and the apostrophe are symbols just like the numbers changed in form to increase the difficulty. But why make it so difficult to decode? And why write it in code in the first place?

Adam clearly felt the need to write down the name of his suspected would-be killer – assuming that is what this sheet contains. Masters would proceed on that assumption since it *was* the tab title of the manila folder in which it was found. Still, Adam did not want his information easily available to anyone who might rifle his desk or safe or wherever he would choose to put the information. If he did know who was making the threats he might have also known it was someone who was skilled at code cracking so he had felt the need to use, or more likely invent, a difficult code - yet still one not so difficult that it could not be broken in case he was killed before he had revealed the person's identity.

And so there it was. After just a few minutes of approaching it as if it were a cryptogram – each number representing a given letter of the alphabet – he had to agree with Millie's earlier conclusion – it was not a simple substitution code. In support of that there was the stand alone letter (4) which could not be either an "A" or "I" - the only two single letter words in English - because of the fourth word group. There are no three letter words beginning with double "A" or double "I".

The use of numbers further complicated the problem. With only ten single digits, including zero, there could not be a one for one substitution for each of the 26 letters in the alphabet. If one assumed the dot and the apostrophe were meant to represent individual letters just as the numbers did, then the number of different letter possibilities was increased from ten to twelve. There had been only nine letters used in the first threat, so that seemed a possibility. It did, however, seem fruitless for anyone other than an expert to pursue it, so Masters moved on to other things.

He reached for the phone beside his chair. "Green button then 6-7. I can do that." And he did.

"Raggs here."

"Raggs, Ray."

"Yes, Sir, how can I be of assistance?"

"I need directions to Alex's studio."

"It is the second door to the right of the study door on the second floor. The first you would probably recognize as a linen closet. May I take you?"

"No. Thank you. Like you, I believe I can distinguish it from a linen closet."

"By the way, Mr. Masters, lunch will be served at twelve o'clock in the dining room – that is on the first floor to the left of the stairs – just opposite from the sitting room actually. Will you be joining us?"

"Yes. Thank you. It's what now? About eleven thirty."

"Eleven thirty four."

"I thought that's what I said." Masters chuckled as he hung up the phone.

Still chuckling, he made his way to the elevator and soon was at the door of the studio. It was open. He knocked on the door frame.

"It's Ray Masters," he called.

"Mr. Masters. Come in. I must say I've been expecting you."

It was a cheery greeting from Alex who offered a hardy hand shake.

"This is my world, Ray."

He extended his arm as he turned, introducing his realm.

"Open. Light. Large. Impressive," Masters said.

"I always hated walls. I like expanses. Hate anything that hems me in. Refused to wear clothes 'til I was six – whenever I could get away with it at least. Sneak in here when the door's closed and you're still likely to find me painting in my natural state."

"I suppose that would qualify you as a genuine art *buff*, then, wouldn't it."

"Mr. Masters! You're not the stuffy old recluse I expected. What can I do you for? Come over by the window and have a seat. Coffee? Tea? Vanilla extract? Don't mind me. I'm a bit near the edge and have always enjoyed just teetering there."

Masters sat and listened, intrigued by the man's incessant chatter. He had to wonder if it was his normal approach to things or a nervous reaction to the visitor at hand.

Alex picked up a remote control and began pressing buttons. Presently a large toy truck headed toward them across the floor. He steered it over a pile of books, backed it into a narrow opening between the sofa and a magazine rack and ran it full speed crashing into the far wall – apparently seeing some humor in that as it lay there on its side, spinning its wheels helplessly.

"It's the kid in me, I guess. Love these gadgets."

When there was a break in the monologue, Masters spoke.

"You said you were expecting me?"

"Interrogation. Bright light. Bamboo shoots under the nails. You know - the usual detective stuff."

"Afraid my visit will disappoint you. I come unarmed."

"I'll just have to spill my guts without intimidation, then. No, I don't know who killed Adam – that's my subtle way of also telling you that I didn't do it, you see. Yes, I do know a dozen – make that ten dozen – people who would have gladly killed him – and one of them probably did. No, I wasn't surprised that it happened; only that it took so damn many years to occur. Yes, I will inherit a bundle and so will my mother. Yes, I will enjoy all that money, particularly because Adam will no longer be able to be enjoying it himself. No, I don't believe it was the butler, but then you can never be sure about the English, can you old chap. (His accent was quite good.) And yes, it is my usual style to commandeer every conversation like this so no one else can put me on the spot, one up me, or require me to respond to their own inane ramblings. My shrink loved it. She raked in a hundred and fifty bucks an hour and never had to say a word. I am fully self-centered and know better than to try and establish a meaningful relationship with a woman. Am I capable of love?

Yes. Do I let myself? Infrequently and most guardedly. Am I uneasy in your presence? I'm scared enough to wet my pants – another good reason not to be wearing any."

"I'm a pussycat, Alex," Masters said. "Anybody who knows me will tell you that."

"A pussycat who's brought down the smartest and most vicious criminals of the past forty years, the way I hear it."

"So *that's* what's giving you *paws* about just being yourself around me."

"I can't believe this. The most respected detective in the country a pun addict - and not a really good one at that."

"There, see. Nothing to be concerned about. Ray Masters, regular Joe."

"Okay. What's on your mind? I'll try to behave now."

"I really just came to see your studio and get a sneak preview of the newest addition to your *Christmas Village Collection* – I get mine every year – probably own at least a square foot of this place by now."

"Really? You like my stuff? My goodness. Who'd a thought? Sure. Come with me."

He led Masters to a far corner. "This is where the genius plays in clay all day."

"And this is your newest creation?" Masters asked.

"Not happy with it – just doesn't seem to work - so probably not one you'll see this year."

"It's just the roofline. See here," Masters said, pointing. "Lift the edges like you did on the '92 General Store. It'll make a great place for one of your elves to perch."

Alex stood back and took a long look. He sat down and took a sharp wooden shaper in hand and began to work.

"Like this, you mean?"

"Yes. I'd have gone deeper but your way looks better."

"A good eye, Ray. Which elf?"

"Slumps, I think. His sagging shoulders and silly grin will complement the new gable line."

"What's your consultation fee? I've been brooding over this all week."

“One free *Alexander Original* should cover things.”

“One free for the next fifty Christmases will be more like it. Where did you come by such a good eye?”

“I sculpt a bit myself. Just for relaxation. I make no pretense of being any good. If I had to be good it wouldn’t be fun anymore.”

“I hear that. It’s why I paint, but don’t sell them. Well, partly that and partly because I just enjoy looking at beautiful, naked female models.”

“So you don’t enjoy working in clay, anymore?” Masters asked.

“Oh, yes. It’s my first love. It’s like I’m a hypocrite about it, though. I hate the way Christmas has become commercialized and yet here I am living off of it myself.”

Masters listened without comment and began looking through the equipment and tools on the table.

“You cut your clay slabs with fishing line, I see.”

“Ya. It’s how I was first taught. Nothing magical about it. And you?”

“I hack off chunks with an old ax. Nothing magical about that either, but fishing line always cuts into my hands.”

“Here’s the secret. Wrap each end around a short dowel like these. Then your hands only touch the wood and not the line.”

“You use this thick line? Looks strong enough to hall in a shark.”

“Got that by mistake some time ago. Your right it would be really hard to use. If you have any use for it, it’s yours.”

“Not really. Thanks for the tour. Now I can brag to my neighbors that I visited the one and only *Alexander* in his private studio. I’ll be the hero of Bingo Night.”

Alex didn’t buy the ‘good ole boy’ routine but let it go.

“Since you’re a fellow sculptor, you might be interested in a life size bronze casting I’m doing for a spa in California. Over here. I’ve just finished a one third size mock up. Easier to work out the design kinks in something this size. I may have to start over with the whole concept, though."

"Oh, Why? It's simply beautiful. A bashful nude, legs together and slightly bent to the left, her head looking down to the right, with long flowing hair following her contours right down to her clearly coy, foot on top of foot, stance."

"It's that single foot – ankle really – where it attaches to the base. I'm afraid it will break at that point. It will only be the thickness of an ankle and in brass this will be one heavy sucker life size. Now I wish that during my course in *Engineering for the Sculpture* I'd have paid less attention to the girls in my class and more to what the instructor had to say."

"I'm sure you can find a structural engineer close by to do your calculations."

"Ya. I just don't like anybody messing with in work – present company clearly excepted. Dumb I suppose but I'm basically a loaner, especially when it comes to my art."

"Well, I hope you work it out. It is a magnificent piece. I suppose I've badgered you enough for now. I had better be getting on. I understand lunch is at noon. You be there?"

"Seldom eat lunch. Mill is always good for a snack later on if I get the munchies."

"By the way," Masters pointed out, "I noticed the alarm clock on your work bench has stopped, just in case you count on it to be accurate."

"Only use it for timing plaster of Paris, but thanks."

"That must be the largest old fashioned alarm clock I've ever seen."

"I need a clock with a big face so I can read it from across the room. Don't dare let that plaster set even a minute too long, you know, or it's impossible to remove cleanly from the mold."

Masters reached out to heft it. It was secured to the table top by two bolts. Masters frowned a clear question. Alex provided an answer.

"When I'm pounding the clay, things tend to jiggle their way off the table. That happened to my old clock once too often. It fell to its death a week or so ago, so I got this new one and bolted it in place. That sucker won't fall, I'll guarantee you that!"

Masters smiled, nodded and left. It had been a strange encounter. He had to wonder which Alex was the real Alex. He could understand how having a strong, unbending father like Adam might have caused Alex to feel intimidated when in the presence of other men of strong reputation. It had been Masters' understanding, however, that Alex had never bent to his father's callous, abusive, personality. Perhaps it had been an act for Masters' benefit, but why? To what end?

Masters made his way directly to the dining room following the unmistakable aroma of broth stock. Millie had a spread of cold cuts, a variety of breads, homemade vegetable soup and an assortment of fruits and puddings. Lunch was a come-when-you're-moved-to-do-so affair and seemed to be available between noon and one. Millie and Raggs were sitting together at a small table in the rear of the room. The larger, round table in the center was set but empty. Masters filled a plate and joined them.

"Dorothy and Betty will be down any moment if you'd rather sit with them at the main table," Millie said as if some kind of requirement of position.

"Restrain your reservations, Miss Millie. If the man wants to enjoy our sparkling wit and fascinating conversation, just let him!" Raggs teased, pulling out a chair.

"And those were my exact reasons for approaching you," Masters said, extending the fun.

"Any luck on the numbers?" Masters asked Millie.

"None. Well other than to be sure it's far more sophisticated than a run of the mill cryptogram."

"I came to the same conclusion. I'm hoping Officer Killroy has been able to find a professional to assist us."

A strange glance passed between the other two.

"What?" Masters had to ask.

"Well," Millie began. "K. Roy Killroy is something of a ..."

Raggs filled her hesitation. "Joke! It's not that he's

stupid it's just that he has no common sense about him – no sense of the present."

"And no social graces," Millie added.

"But he *is* a detective on the police force. He can't be totally inept."

"Well, yes he can be, honey," Millie answered, patting Masters hand, compassion plain in her tone. "His grandfather is a political powerhouse in these parts so when Roy expressed a interest in police work he was suddenly our newest detective. Been at for twenty some years now. He gets shoved from one unimportant assignment to another. I'm sure his superiors felt the meeting today was one of those and so Roy got it."

"He is a well meaning sort," Raggs added as if to cushion the bluntness of his former statements. "Wouldn't hurt a fly. Doesn't seem to have many friends. Came here several months ago on a burglary case. We were nice to him. He just kept coming back. We couldn't get rid of him. He hung on and hung on."

"How did you end it?"

"Mr. W. called somebody and it was suddenly all over," Millie explained. "Mr. W. had friends in high places."

"About the many faces of Alex," Masters began.

"Did he hit you with his *'Babble on Alex'* or his *'Too Depressed to Breath'* Alex?"

"The former, I guess. Is that for real?"

"Comes and goes," Millie answered. "Mostly with strangers – celebrated strangers, and there have been lots of them walk these halls. I think it's how he handles his inferiority feelings."

"That and just staying to himself," Raggs added.

They continued to eat and talk about more mundane topics. Millie still needed a seven letter word for *shabby* – Masters supplied three possibilities - "*Scruffy, Unkempt, Rumpled.*" It turned out to be the first. Raggs put in several requests for Sunday dinner – yams, ham, and bread pudding. Masters suddenly hoped the case didn't get solved too soon.

"When Officer Killroy arrives we will need access to

the attic. It's through the handyman's room you said. Guy . . ."

"... Lester. Guy Lester. Been here forever it seems," came Raggs' response.

"He came soon after Dorothy and Mr. Williams were married," Millie said to clarify the timeline. "He's a nice man. Keeps mostly to himself."

"Competent. Hard working. He never causes any problems. Often takes his meals in his room," were Raggs final comments.

Not stellar recommendations but the man seemed to have found his niche and apparently got on well enough with the family and fellow employees.

"I have yet to meet him," Masters said.

"Working on the back roof this morning. Cleaning the gutters before the snows arrive, I suppose," Raggs explained. "He knows this house inside and out. If you have any questions about it, he'll have the answers. He's the one who installed the chandelier. Must have been - what, Millie - fifteen years ago?"

"About that, I'd say."

Raggs excused himself to assist Dorothy and Betty as they arrived. Masters took advantage of his absence to inquire further about him. "Raggs wife?"

"Lost her to cancer years ago. Doesn't speak of her. Still madly in love with her, I'd say. It's his one down side. Everything else is upbeat. Sad to see someone grieve for so long about something that's done and over."

"Yes, I'd say so," Masters said. "He intrigues me, I guess."

"How's that?"

"He is clearly well educated and yet a life-long butler."

"He don't talk much about himself. Here's what I've pieced together. He came from a servant class sort a family north of London – that's in England. He was in his third year of college when his father died under mysterious circumstances - I may be telling you more than I know, there, but that's how it seems to me. Anyway, he had to drop out of school and support his mother. That's how he got into the butler line of work I think – it's what his father did. After his mother died, he married – they had a boy that's the apple of his eye."

"Yes, Raggs mentioned him to me."

"I don't know much more about him. After his wife died he ended up here – maybe a clean break with his old life, you know."

"I see. Any idea about what he was studying in college?"

"Engineering, I believe. Doesn't strike me as the engineer type, you know. He can change a light bulb all by himself."

She chuckled. It had clearly been a reference to the joke about how many engineers it takes to change that device. She continued.

"About the only engineer part of him left I guess is that metal detector he loves to play with. Always out here and there searching for buried this and that."

"Well, like I said, he's an intriguing person."

Masters was ready to close the conversation and pushed back from the table.

Millie, clearly a bright person herself, felt the need to pull Masters' chain just ever so slightly:

"I'm afraid that when you get Raggs to open up about *me*, you won't find nearly so much to talk about. I was born, dropped out of high school, became a maid and spent most a my life right here."

She chuckled into her hands as Masters stood. Taken off guard, no ready comeback came to mind.

"I'll take care of the plate, Mr. M. It's what I get the big bucks for."

She continued giggling her wonderful giggle and motioned Masters to be on his way.

Masters made appointments with Dotty and Betty for later in the day.

Killroy arrived. Masters then commandeered Raggs. "Do you have time now to get us into the attic?"

"Certainly."

A short elevator ride later and they were at Guy's door.

Raggs knocked. It was immediately answered by a slender man in his early sixties. He had a weathered, deeply tanned face and sandy hair - gray only at the temples. He wore loose jeans, a long sleeved red flannel shirt and work boots. He demonstrated little expression either on his face or in his tone.

"Yes?" It was more an inquiry than a greeting. He directed the comment to Raggs but then looked Masters up one side and down the other.

"This is detective Raymond Masters, Mr. Lester. He is looking into the death of Mr. Williams. He needs access to the attic and I told him that your knowledge of the house and especially of the chandelier would be invaluable to him. You remember Detective Killroy."

Guy unchained the door and opened it. He turned and pointed to the ceiling near the east wall of his large room.

"The pull-down stairs are there. I'll get 'em set."

As he unfolded them, Masters glanced around the sizeable room. Two large windows across the back and the West sides should have added a bright, cheery look to the room. They didn't. It was furnished with an odd assortment of large pieces - a four poster bed in one corner, a kitchen area with microwave, refrigerator, cabinets and sink in the northwest rear corner, a sitting area with a small TV toward the front of the inside wall and a large workshop area behind that in the Northeast corner. Masters assumed that the two undersized doors in the east wall near the rear led to the bathroom and a closet. The large couch had to be moved several feet in order for the stairs to be unfolded suggesting they were not used frequently.

Guy looked at Masters and then at the stairs.

"I think they'll hold you," came his indelicate but all quite serious and honest evaluation.

"Perhaps if I empty my pockets" Masters said, hoping to lighten the situation. Raggs snickered. Killroy stood silent. It seemed to pass over Guy's head or at least his interest. He went first.

"Any further need for my services, Mr. Masters?" Raggs asked.

"Well, yes, actually. I'd like you to come on up with us if you have time. You may have some information that will be helpful."

It was clear that Raggs didn't fully understand what that might mean but he was inquisitive by nature and brightened at the invitation.

The attic was unfinished with bare joists and two foot wide, bare wood walkways set in place running here and there. A thick layer of dust blanketed the poured, rock-wool insulation that had settled low between the massive beams.

"I'm most interested in the connection to the chandelier," Masters said.

Guy pointed and led the way. The area was well lit by a series of bare bulbs in very old, white porcelain sockets attached to the rafters. The double, black wires connecting them suggested they were probably original accessories.

The roof area over the opening to the chandelier came to a pointed peak and provided more than ample standing room. The area around the opening was floored. There was a metal collar anchored to that floor. A metal pipe, three inches in diameter, was welded to the collar and rose to a height of twelve inches. There was a three quarter inch hole in each side of the pipe about six inches from the floor. Matching holes in the central pipe on the fallen chandelier had fit there and a strong metal rod had run through them from east to west securing the huge light fixture in place. The collar was empty and the rod gone.

"Have you been up here since the chandelier fell?" Masters asked Guy.

"No," came his short and complete answer.

"Tell me what you see here that's not as it should be?" Masters asked.

Guy's answer was thoughtful and deliberate.

"The upper end of the chandelier has fallen away. The

electrical wires have snapped but are still fed down through the collar. The rod that supported the chandelier has been removed. That's it laying over there."

"Can you conceive of any way in which that rod could have slipped out of place and ended up over there without human assistance?"

"No."

"I understand you installed the fixture yourself."

"Yes."

"Will you explain how that was done?"

"It set on the floor down in the study. I fastened a block and tackle to the rafters up here right above the hole." He pointed to a horizontal 2 x 4 bolted in place near the peak. "I fed a rope through the pipe down into the study and tied it to the chandelier. Pulled it up into place, put the rod through the holes and completed the wiring."

"And the block and tackle was then removed," Masters commented.

Guy took that as a statement not needing his confirmation or response. Masters proceeded.

"The block and tackle had been attached to this substantial cross beam between the rafters, is that correct?" Masters asked, adding the specific question to be answered.

"Ya. You can see the notch I cut in the top to keep the hook stable and in the exact right place."

"The hook that held the block and tackle?" Masters asked.

Guy nodded. Masters examined the notch.

"Look at the notch if you will and tell me what seems wrong with it today."

Guy's face clouded, not fully understanding the request but obliged the old man. His face lit up.

"Why, there ain't a speck of dust in it. The top of the rest of the two by four is a quarter inch thick with dust but there ain't none in the groove."

He nodded toward Masters as if finally giving him his approval. Raggs looked from the other side and spoke.

"Also, there seem to be some fibers in the edge of the groove back here," he said. "Looks like from a rope to me."

Masters and Guy moved so they could take a look. Masters carefully removed several strands and put them in a small plastic bag taken from his own jacket pocket and handed them to Killroy.

"Good eyes, Raggs."

"Important?" Guy asked, for the first time showing some genuine interest in the activity.

"They look fresh. It means a rope was recently used here - probably to support the chandelier while the rod was removed. The question is, how did it remain in place without the rod or was the rod left in place until the final second and then removed by someone up here in the attic."

"Quite a mystery," Killroy added trying to be a part of it all.

Raggs spoke.

"Seems quite possible that a rope was fastened to the chandelier with a bow knot and the rod removed. The rope would have been its only support. Then, a simple tug on the loose end of the rope would untie it and allow it to fall."

"A better theory than mine," Masters said.

"There's problems with both of them," Guy offered.

"What's that?" Masters asked pleased that Guy was entering into the inspection.

"The stairs have a lock on them. I have the only key and it stays on my key ring. So, nobody but me could have been up here, and I wasn't. I was out on the roof."

"And nobody has borrowed them?"

"Well, I suppose they have in the past, but usually if somebody needs a lock opened I just go do it for them."

"Actually," Raggs began, "I borrowed the key ring about ten days ago, myself. There was a trickle of water coming out from under a locked door in the basement and I wanted to investigate. Guy was busy with something else and lent me the key ring."

"That's right. One of the old pipes sprang a leak. Good

thing you found it when you did. I got it patched later that day."

"Can you remember loaning them out to anybody else?"

"Well, yes, now that I start thinking about it. Mr. Williams needed them when he lost his garage key - that was probably three weeks ago. How far back should I go?"

"Oh, a month or so for now."

"Alex has a attic area up above his studio. It's separated from this area by that stone fire wall there." He pointed to the east wall. "He stores stuff up there he doesn't use anymore. Alex is the worst about losing things. I guess that would have been maybe six weeks ago or a little less that he couldn't find his key and needed to borrow mine. The next day I had a copy made for him. Nothing else comes to mind right now. I'll keep thinking."

"The lock on his side takes a different key from this one?" Masters asked.

"I ain't certain now that you ask. I got different keys on my ring but I guess I just never compared them. I'll do that."

With considerable effort and great care, Masters got down on his hands and knees in order to get a closer look at the metal collar itself.

"Looks like fresh grease in the East hole. Would that be something you've put here recently, Mr. Lester?"

"No. Never, in fact."

"Look over here in the other hole. What do you make of that?"

Guy and Raggs both knelt down to take a look. (Masters took note of how much easier that act seemed for them than it had been for him!)

"Looks like splinters of wood," Raggs said.

"Ya. That's wood splinters alright," Guy agreed

Killroy bent deeply from the waist and nodded his confirmation from three feet away.

"Masters took out his pad and began drawing a diagram of the collar."

Raggs watched.

"If I might, Sir," he said, interrupting the process. I may be just a bit more skilled at such things."

He reached – somewhat tentatively - for Masters' pad and pencil. Masters offered them to him without hesitation. Raggs had been right. His drawing could have come right from an architect's table.

"Show the grease and the splinters. They seem to be held in place by the grease," Masters said upon further observation.

The men stood up.

"No way the electrical cables could have supported the chandelier is there?" Masters asked Guy.

"No, Sir. Not a chance. There was probably four extra feet of slack in them. By the time it fell that far its weight would a snapped them like string."

"Raggs examined the dangling ends of the wires and nodded his silent agreement with Guy's analysis."

That had been Masters' first impression as well, but verification was useful.

Guy spotted it first.

"That don't belong here," he said pointing to a wire stretched out on the insulation just to the west of the floor area around the chandelier opening. He bent down to pick it up but then hesitated, looking at Masters as if for permission.

"Yes. Let's see what it is."

Guy searched out the near end and held it under a light where they could all see it. Attached to end of the wire, through a small hole, was a piece of wood - a foot long, nearly three quarters of an inch square. The end opposite the wire had been badly splintered.

"It wasn't broken in two as if cracked over someone's knee," Master observed. "It's more as if it were just sheered off – scraping against something."

Guy pointed to the grease near the splintered end. "It's long enough to go through the holes where the rod was supposed to be but it sure ain't strong enough to hold the weight of the chandelier. It would have snapped in two as soon as the full weight was put on it."

"And," Masters pointed out, "The grease is only on one end. If it had been through both holes there would be grease on both ends and probably in between. Let's see where the other end of the wire leads us?"

Guy carefully followed the wire without moving it. It headed straight for the back wall. He took a flashlight from his tool belt and lit the area near the open joists where it appeared to stop. He bent to his knees to examine it further.

"What do you find?" Masters asked, hesitant to attempt walking the beams in that unfloored area.

"Beats all," Guy began. "There's a half inch pipe stuck clean through the wall - through the mortar between the blocks - to the outside and the wire goes into it. Must end up outside someplace."

"About where would it come out?" Masters asked.

Guy leaned back, surveying the placement.

"Just above and to the right of the East window on the back wall of my room, I'd say. Somewhere between that one and the little window in my bathroom. Probably three feet above the top of the windows. This old place has those twelve foot ceilings you know."

Masters turned to Raggs.

"Let's draw out the route of the wire and the measurements as accurately as we can estimate them."

Raggs handed the pad to Masters.

"Done, Sir."

"Impressive. Sure you don't moonlight as a private eye?"

"Sounds tempting, but no, Sir. Anticipatory thoroughness. It is a trait that has always stood me in good stead."

They moved back to the opening in the floor.

"There is some important piece missing here," Masters said, looking around.

"What?" Guy asked.

"I have no idea," Masters answered. "It's one of those, *'we'll know it when we find it,'* sort of things."

"If I may, Sir," Raggs asked. "The wire from the stick – if it had been in the collar - had to turn at a 90 degree angle to get to the pipe in the rear wall, so it could have never pulled the stick from the collar. To do that it would have had to pull in a line that went straight west not straight north."

"Good observation," Masters said. "Thank you. Well, I guess we're finished up here for now. I'll undoubtedly want to revisit it."

Masters continued to survey the attic area for several moments.

"That bulb. The one directly over the hole. It appears to be different from the others up here."

Killroy moved to examine it more closely.

"Yes, Sir. It is. One of those new daylight bulbs – sort of purplish in color."

Masters turned to Guy.

"Did you replace a bulb here recently?"

"No. The lights are just never on up here. I don't remember *ever* replacing one, actually."

Masters addressed Killroy.

"Let's get a print man out here and dust that bulb and fixture. Also, have them give this whole area a good going over – the floor around the hole, the collar, the rod, the two-by up there where the notch is, the pipe in the back wall there – anything they see that could hold a print. We'll need that rod. Do you have a large enough evidence bag? Mine are all too small."

Killroy seemed pleased to be able to contribute something substantial and he produced a long narrow bag and secured the rod.

"I'm correct in assuming there is no grease on any part of that rod, right?" Masters asked.

Killroy looked it over.

"That's right. I don't see any grease."

He bagged the rod.

Masters was not quite finished.

"And how about another bag for the stick. If you would

just undo it from the wire, we need to have the lab examine it as well. Try not to leave prints on the stick."

Finished for the time being they returned to Guy's room. Guy swung the stairs back into place. Masters looked puzzled.

"You said the stairs locked - needed a key. I don't see the lock and they are way too high to reach without a ladder."

Guy pointed to a key lock in the wall, nearby.

"Pretty clever, really," he said. "Turn the key to the right and it opens a little electric solenoid up above that usually keeps the stair casing locked in place - a spring loaded gadget like on the old fashioned pinball machines. Now, I'll turn it back to the left and it will release the solenoid pin back into place and the stairs are locked up tighter than a drum."

"Yes, I'd say *quite* clever. I have to wonder why one would want an attic stairway locked in the first place."

"Maybe to keep little kids from going up there," Guy said more like a concerned father than a handyman.

Masters nodded then asked, "Do these back windows open? I'd like to see if we can find where that wire comes out and where it goes."

"Sure do."

Guy opened the window and locked it in place.

"With these solid stone walls, the windows have to be held up with these little slide locks. It couldn't be built with the rope and weight systems usually used in wooden construction back then."

He looked outside.

"It's hanging down right here within easy reach. Take a look."

Masters examined the arrangement. A piece of wood with the wire secured to its center appeared to be a handle. Pull the wire at that spot and it easily moved through the pipe back to the stick that had been attached to the other end up in the attic.

"Would you hear someone if they were up above walking around?" Masters asked.

"I'm not sure. Never had that happen, I guess," Guy

answered.

"Would you mind going back up and moving about so I can see what amount of noise it makes?"

"No problem. Beats being outside on the roof cleaning gutters in his weather."

It was as close to humor as the man had come.

Guy lowered the stairs and was soon moving around up above. There were occasional creaks but nothing that would have signaled a person's presence up there.

Masters realized that it may have been an exercise in futility anyway, since the only access to that section of the attic was by way of those stairs, and if Guy had been in the room to hear someone moving about above him, he would have also had to know who had climbed the stairs to get there. Unless, of course, that person was Guy, himself. If it had been Guy, however, he had just done a superb job of covering for himself.

If it had not been Guy, the attic work would have had to have been done when Guy was elsewhere and by someone with a copy of the key. To that point in the investigation it seemed that other person could have been either Raggs or Alex and of course Adam, but that possibility seemed irrelevant.

Masters also understood it could be that Guy and somebody else could have been in on the plan together. Once Masters figured out just how the release of the chandelier had been triggered, he felt he would probably be in a better position to know who was involved. Nothing he had seen upstairs seemed right - the wooden replacement rod, the hole in the wall, or the wire. The important questions were; 'If none of that made sense, then why was it there; what was its purpose? And where were the things that would make sense?'

Masters thanked Guy and Raggs for their assistance. He and Killroy then went to the study, next door. Masters examined the chandelier which had not been moved from where it had come to rest on the floor behind the desk, after hitting Adam. He looked at the end of the central pipe that fit up into the collar in the attic. There were traces of grease in and around both holes and, as he had suspected there would be, wood fragments in one of them.

"Detective would you be able to scrape these wood splinters from this hole into an evidence bag for us?" Masters asked. "And be sure to designate which hole."

Killroy set to work.

"What do you estimate this fixture weighs?" Masters asked, as much to himself as Killroy.

Killroy looked it over and tapped on the metal rings that held the light fixtures in five successively smaller circles toward the lower end. He counted the individual bulbs and began speaking.

"Well, fifty sockets at say eight ounces each and another eight for each bulb would be fifty pounds. Wrought iron rings a half inch thick and six inches high. Range from about four feet in diameter down to one foot. Probably another three hundred pounds there. The metal rods that attach the rings to the central pipe and that pipe itself – I'd say add another fifty pounds easy. What's that about four hundred pounds? Gee's, that's like having a piano fall on you."

Killroy's estimation was a bit lighter than Masters' but still in the ballpark. Either way, it represented instant death if it hit you on the head. That raised another question. It seemed to have had the end of the pipe aimed directly at where Adam's head would be. He verified that by sighting straight up from the center of Adam's chair.

"Detective, if you were trying to learn whether or not this desk had been moved recently, what would you look for?"

"Marks in the carpet I suppose – where the legs had been setting."

"And looking at this carpet, what would your conclusion be?"

Killroy looked from several positions before answering

"It's been moved several feet away from the back wall where it had been sitting."

"That verifies Raggs' earlier conclusion. Contact your print guys and see what they have on the bulbs and desk. "

"I'll put in a call right now."

While Killroy made the call, Masters went next door to the studio. The door was open. Alex was working at his clay table in the rear of the large room. As he had done before, Masters knocked on the door frame and Alex swiveled on his stool, motioning him to come in.

By the time he reached Alex, the artist had turned back to his work.

"Making a rubber mold. I assume that means you're finally satisfied with your creation," Masters said.

"Oh, I may go through this a half dozen times before the final product."

"How does the process work, if I'm not too nosey?"

"No. Always glad to share my trade secrets with fellow artisans. First, I make an oversized model of the building and work out the problems. Then I make a final size version, like this one. I work in self-hardening clay with a low shrink ratio. When the surface is dry to the touch I apply this latex rubber with a brush – about ten coats to make a good thick, tough, flexible mold. I add some fibers around the corners to keep it from ballooning when it's filled. Once dry, I remove the original and clean out the mold. Then I make a plaster of Paris casting. A half hour later I have my first solid little building – it's like fathering a child. I fill any imperfections on the surface and sand any rough spots. When I get a casting I think is perfect I get it ready to ship to the company that makes the final molds and does the final castings in ceramic. Then I make several more from my latex mold and paint them. When I get the colors just right, I ship it off to them, too, so their artists will know exactly how it is to be painted. They cast them, paint them, glaze them, and market them while I sit here painting beautiful women and raking in the wampum. Probably the cushiest job in the universe."

He put his brush in water and turned to Masters.

"I imagine that you really didn't come here for a lecture on something I'm sure you already knew about."

Masters nodded somewhat sheepishly.

"There are a couple of questions I thought you might be

able to help clear up."

"Shoot."

Alex stood and walked toward the sitting area. Masters followed.

"A drink?" Alex asked.

"No thank you, but go ahead if you like."

"Too early for booze. Diet soda gives you brain tumors and the chlorine in this water's enough to kill you. I'll pass, too, I guess."

They sat and Masters began.

"About the recent carpet shampooing?"

"Shampooing off schedule, you mean?"

"Well, yes, actually. I understand you took it upon yourself to order that done, and I get the idea that kind of initiative is, how can I say . . . unusual?"

"You are a man of great tact, Mr. Masters. "Unusual would be an understatement. You want the long or short version?"

"The succinctly accurate version."

"First time you've actually sounded like a Harvard man."

"I hope you'll forgive me."

Alex just smiled and began his explanation.

"When Adam is away I get a kick out of spending time in his study doing all the things I know he'd hate if he knew I was doing them."

"Such as?" Masters asked, both amused and intrigued.

"Rearranging the books on his shelves, prying open his desk drawers and mixing papers between folders, sitting in his chair with my bare feet on his desk, smoking the most disgusting cigars I can find – just playful little things like that. I know he knows that I'm the culprit but he has never once mentioned it too me. Well, a week ago I was in there sitting in his chair oiling my new boots. Somehow in the process I dumped over a quart of oil and it splattered ten feet across his carpet. Now, I do things that I hope will irritate the hell of him but I've never been destructive – I'm not that kind of a person.

So, I had the carpet cleaned. It may seem like a lame story but it's the truth."

"I'll accept that. I am mostly interested in why the desk was not put back in its usual place."

"It wasn't? I didn't know that. I don't know – well, maybe. You see, the usual cleaners weren't available on such short notice, so I found another crew to come in. They'd never done it before. I suppose they just weren't careful and didn't put it back right. Maybe Raggs knows something about it. He was in and out of there several times while they were working on it."

"I appreciate your help. I'll do that. I'll ask Raggs. Thanks for the suggestion."

Masters noticed a chess set on a table near a window.

"You're a chess player, I see"

"A little. Not a student of the game. Just for pleasure."

"Me too. We could probably bore each other into a draw in no time."

"Perhaps we'll find time to match wits," Alex said.

"Perhaps," Masters said and left.

He met Raggs at the bottom of the stairs. There was a message from Guy.

"Guy asked that I tell you that the two attic entrances do take different keys."

"I suspected as much. Thank you."

"Your belongings have been gathered and put in your quarters. Would you like to examine them?"

"I'm sure they are fine, but yes, I'd like to see my room, and get out of this monkey suit and into something more comfortable. I am to speak with Dotty at two. Where would you suggest?"

"Dotty particularly likes the sitting room. I can't imagine why – it's perfectly dreadful – but yes, the sitting room I believe. I'll see that she knows."

Chapter Three:
Day one: Mid-afternoon

The suite looked comfortable – bedroom, sitting area, huge closet, and a bathroom large enough to accommodate a game with the Harlem Globetrotters. There were lightly draped windows across the East wall, which led him to believe he must be on the outside wall directly below Alex's studio. Masters shed his coat and tie in favor of a cardigan. At two o'clock he headed for the sitting room.

Dorothy was already there.

"Hope I haven't made you wait long," Masters said, taking a seat across a coffee table from where she was sitting on a small, red satin, love seat. The room was in the front of the house and had three large windows on the south and east walls. They were draped in heavy, dark green, shiny fabric and topped with overbearing, matching, cornices. The treatment presented no real contrast to the equally dark green, flocked, papered wall above the dark mahogany wainscoting, which maintained a strangle hold on the lower three feet of the room. The floors were dark wood and there were a dozen small throw rugs here and there around the room. The furniture was mostly Victorian in style but much of it had been reupholstered in more modern looking fabrics, perhaps in an unsuccessful attempt to add some brightness to an otherwise thoroughly cheerless room. If this was Dorothy's favorite spot, the rest of the house must have been abysmal.

She smiled across at Masters.

"I came a bit early. I like to just sit in here. It's a grand place to think. There's nothing remotely pleasant here to distract you."

Her remark answered Masters' unasked question.

"How are you doing?" Masters asked, immediately realizing what a shallow beginning that had been.

"Well it's a terrible thing to say, but I'm more upset by all the paperwork I'm about to have to undertake than I am about his death. We hadn't been close for years. I suppose you know about his women. He supported me very well and I guess that was meant to make up for the rest. It didn't but perhaps now it will."

"You'll stay here?"

"I'm not sure. Alex says make a clean break. Sell the place and find exactly what I want somewhere in a more moderate climate. Problem is I have never allowed myself to think about what I would really like so I have no good ideas."

"Perhaps that can be an enjoyable and exciting undertaking during the next few months."

"Perhaps. Now, how can I help you?"

"I'm not sure. I was hoping you might have thought of some things by now. My first impression is that it was probably an inside job."

"Someone here in this household?" Dorothy asked, appearing shocked.

"In terms of knowing people's schedules and gaining access to the attic, it seems that way. But then, I have only begun. Could we suspect either Millie or Raggs?"

"Oh, goodness no! I mean they both hated it when Adam would go off on Alex or me and they both urged me to make my own life outside this place, but to kill Adam – I hardly think so.

"Adam and Millie even had what might be considered a positive relationship. They tormented each other with their skill at decoding cryptograms. On his last birthday, Millie gave him a book of the *Thousand Toughest Cryptograms* – or some such title. She had cut the answer section out of it. You can bet she did it to taunt him. There is some imp in her! He, of course, took it as an indication of her respect for his skill. What a pair."

"And you? Are you a cryptogrammer?" Masters asked.

"Oh yes. Cryptograms, crosswords, word searches – anything and everything to fill my dreary hours. I even read trashy romances and Garrison Flint books. Well, that didn't come out entirely as I intended. [I would hope not!] Anyway, because of those books, I do feel like I know and can trust you, Mr. Masters." [You're welcome.]

"I'm honored. Let's move on to Guy."

"Guy. Yes. Well, he's another story which means you need to know even another story first."

Masters settled back in his chair, puzzled but prepared to listen.

"I haven't spoken of these things to anyone before. I ask that you only reveal what you must during the course of your investigation."

Masters nodded.

"Adam was not Alexander's father. His father was a young man named Peter Lassiter. I was twenty and madly in love with Peter. Adam had wanted me to date him since my freshman year in college - we had a class together. He was persistent and we went out several times. His expensive car, a chauffer, flowers, presents – he swept me off my feet. It was Peter I loved but Adam who I wanted. Quite a dilemma for a middleclass girl from Elgin.

"Peter was from a poor family in a predominately Italian area of south Chicago. He had worked hard since he'd been fourteen, helping to support his mother and younger brother. He kept bad company but he was a good boy. Undesirable friends were the only ones available where he lived.

"One night there was a liquor store robbery in Peter's

neighborhood and two employees were killed. There were three eyewitnesses who identified Peter as the one of the three robbers who had the gun. He was arrested, tried and convicted – all in a matter of months. Of course none of his so-called friends came forward to help. Neither of the other two was ever found.

"To this day I don't believe Peter did it but he was poor and had been in lots of trouble as a juvenile. The authorities needed to make an example of somebody in an attempt to control the rampant, hoodlum crime in that area of South Chicago. They asked for the death penalty and got it. While he was awaiting appeal he was killed in prison by another inmate. His killer was never apprehended.

"I found myself pregnant by Peter and courted by Adam so I agreed to marry Adam for the child's sake. Adam was charming and wealthy and I figured he would provide things for my baby that my family and I never could, and he has – I'll give him that much.

"Alex was born seven months after our wedding. We told everyone he was premature. We just didn't take him out in public for several months. It would have been hard to pass off an eight pound five ounce baby as premature."

"Does Alex know?"

"No. I've never told him. It was always so hard to know what was right. Adam convinced me it would damage the boy to know that he had a murderer for a father. I gave in and just left it at that.

"As soon as Alexander was born things changed with Adam. He became distant from me. He set up his own bedroom and soon became short tempered and abusive. He stayed out all night two or three times a week. He never brought his women here. I suppose that's also to his credit in a twisted sort of way.

"At one point, when Alexander was seven, things got so bad with Adam that I told him I was leaving. He said if I did he would tell Alexander about his father and point out to him all the similar, criminal-like traits he had, and make it sound like they were clearly inherited from Peter. I didn't know what else to do so I stayed – succumbed might better describe it. Adam was so strong and I was so weak. It has not been a happy life, Mr. Masters.

"Once Alexander became old enough to be told about his own father - old enough to sift through what was true and not true about himself – I was afraid of what he might do to Adam. Alexander has a short fuse – a learned gift from Adam, no doubt. Well, I didn't say that to make him a suspect. I hadn't even considered it. Oh, my!"

She put her handkerchief to her mouth.

"Never mind about that. You haven't told him about his father so we have no reason to believe he knows. Your story has not implicated him," Masters said, trying to reassure her. "Besides, this was not a crime from a violent temper. This was a very carefully planned and patiently carried out undertaking."

She nodded and patted at the corners of her eyes.

"But all of this must have been the pre-story to the one about Guy," Masters said, hoping to move the conversation on in a helpful direction.

"Oh, yes. Guy. He is Peter's younger brother – Alex's true uncle. He changed his name from Lassiter to Lester – the brother of the infamous Peter Lassiter was not about to be hired in these parts. I convinced Adam to hire him – as Guy Lester. Adam never knew Guy was Peter's brother – at least I don't believe he did."

"The plot thickens as they say," Masters mused.

"From the beginning, Guy feared for my safety. I guess Adam had a reputation - one that I was unaware of - as having a terrible temper and being quite violent toward those who crossed him. As I learned later, his father kept an attorney on retainer just to keep Adam's record clean. So, Guy wanted to be near me to protect me and Alex – Peter had told him I was pregnant with his child. The upshot is, Adam hired Guy and he has been here with us ever since."

"So you and Guy are close?" Masters asked.

"Oh, yes. He has been my rock all these years."

"And Adam knew you were close?"

"No, I don't think so. He never mentioned it. I think if he had thought that Guy and I were friends we'd have had a new handyman in a matter of days. Adam was jealous of any men in my life. We have always been very careful. Adam didn't seem to want me to have a happy life. I always wondered, I suppose, if that was because I had told him I was going to marry Peter – just before the trouble – and he has been punishing me for not choosing him first. Now, I'll surely never know."

"You speak about it all with so little emotion."

"Emotion? My emotions drained away years ago. I probably don't even love Alexander to the extent I should. I suppose I've just also made Guy a suspect, haven't I?"

"You have told me nothing I wouldn't have uncovered with a little more sweat and leg work. What Guy is or isn't, is not of your doing."

"I suppose. I wish I could help with outside suspects – from his business life - but frankly I don't know any of his business associates other than John and he's a lamb. I can't imagine him being a part of killing Adam – though, goodness knows, I suppose he probably had good reason."

"Anything specific?"

"No. Just knowing strong willed Adam and weak spined John, he was bound to have been taken advantage of over the years."

"That leaves just Betty, I guess," Masters said, hoping to bring the conversation to a close.

"Betty. She's put up with the man for the past fifteen years. Once she discovered I knew about Adam's women, we became good friends. She had felt guilty, knowing about them herself, and making arrangements for the rendezvous. We enjoy each others company. When I go out evenings it is usually with her. She never married. Strong minded and independent in her ways. Marriage might not have worked because of it. She seems to know that. She sees men but none for very long. I'm not sure if that is her preference or theirs.

"She has very simple tastes. The *things* in life have never meant much to her even though sometimes she talks as if they do. Her apartment is modest. She doesn't have a lot of clothes. Her car is twelve years old and as long as it runs I'm sure she won't consider buying another one.

"Betty is brilliant. She is far more than a secretary. She ran the business, really. Adam was gone so much buying and selling. I assume he paid her handsomely. He'd have had to in order for her to put up with him. I've asked her to stay on and keep the business together until we can get it sold. I'm sure she and John will do what's best."

"As far as you know then, Betty never meant anything more to Adam than just being an efficient assistant."

"No. I don't think so. No. I hadn't considered it."

"Adam's trips away from home. They were always business?"

"Yes. I'm quite sure about that. I only went on one – it was early in our marriage. We went to London for ten days. Mostly I stayed in the hotel while he was out and about. It wasn't much fun. Alexander was back here with his nanny and Millie. I was mostly alone. One night Adam came in late and asked me – no *told* me – that if the authorities asked where he had been that evening, I was to say that he had been in the room with me the whole time. Gratefully, I was never questioned by anyone. We left the next morning. I hated the idea of lying for him but I knew if he asked that of me I would, so I just never went with him again."

"You say that Guy came soon after you were married. And that Betty came about fifteen years ago. When did Millie and Raggs come?"

"Millie was here when I moved in. She had been here several years. Adam's father had hired her to run the household after his wife died. A year later, he was gone, also. Raggs came a few years after that. We didn't have a Butler before. I'm not sure how all that came to be. Millie says he just sent a letter of application and Adam hired him. You'll have to ask Raggs if you want more details. He has become an irreplaceable part of the household – its very backbone in his quiet sort of way."

"Adam had not spoke to you about the recent death threats?"

"No, but then we didn't speak about anything. I guess he hadn't told anyone. He was a very efficient person. As he said, he called the meeting for this morning so he could inform everyone who needed to know all at the same time – he was most efficient in his self-centered way. Let them all use *their* time to come to him so he could take just five minutes out of his day to tell everyone at once. He was pretty predictable. When he found something that worked he kept with it. He hadn't varied his daily routine around here for years."

"I appreciate your time and your candor, Dorothy. I told Betty I'd be dropping in on her so if you'll excuse me."

"Certainly. I am so glad you are here. Thanks for staying."

She reached out and held his hand for a long moment. Then Masters made his way to Betty's office, a straight shot from the front door, past the east side of the staircase and through a set of mammoth double doors.

"Mr. Masters. Welcome," Betty said, stepping from behind her desk to offer him her hand in a hardy shake.

Masters looked around.

"Who ever designed this house certainly was not stingy with space. What a grand, big, area."

"Grand, big and bleak. It was designed as the Senior Mr. Williams' office. When Adam took over he moved upstairs away from the hubbub. He is – was – always on the phone – didn't like the background noise of a working office. How can I help?"

"You get right to point. I assume that was a trait Mr. Williams could appreciate."

"Oh, yes. The least lost effort the better."

"You seem to be the only real connection there is with the other women in his life. Would you consider any of them suspects in his murder?"

"All of them and none of them."

"Seems to be some lost effort in *that* response."

Betty smiled naturally for the first time.

"Adam used his women and then threw them aside. They all knew it was coming sooner or later so it was never a big surprise. He was not a nice man even to his mistresses. He provided well for them while they were his playthings and because of that, they put up with his demanding, inconsiderate, always be there when I want you, ways. They'll all be happy to hear someone finally cut him down to size. But they'll all be hurting as well. He had a standard severance arrangement with his women. As long as he was alive they would receive a "consultation fee" every month. It varied from girl to girl but was always enough for them to live in style. It may have been less for past services provided than it was to protect his own neck in the future. He knew people hated him. He counted on his ex-women friends to fear him – nixing the blackmail angle."

"So, that's probably a dead end street, you think."

"I'd say so."

"You had said earlier that they were all in his Will."

"What I intended to say was they all *think* they are in his will. It was part of his line. "

"The same for you?"

"No. I have his Will. I typed it every time he made changes. I *know* I'm there and was there long before he required me to be his lady."

"Required?"

"It was an 'or else' dictum. I knew it wouldn't be forever so what the hell. I could have felt guilty. Dorothy and I are friends, but I'm enough like Adam that didn't happen. If not me it would have been somebody else."

"And Dorothy doesn't know?"

"I don't think so. I'd bet that she doesn't?"

"How are you at cryptograms?"

"What a strange question. Pretty good, actually. So

was Adam. Believe it or not, Millie is probably better than either of us?

"And Raggs?"

"Raggs and cryptograms. I have no idea. He's a pretty smart guy. I'm sure he'd be good if he pursued them. I just don't know. I'm still puzzled about the question."

"Adam received three death threats recently - all written as cryptograms - probably by someone who was pretty good at them."

"I see. I didn't know that."

"Apparently no one did. Also, the document Adam had in the folder on his desk was written in code. The folder tab indicated it contained information about who he thought had sent the threats. It is not a typical cryptogram, however. Some other code. One he created, I imagine, but one he felt sure one of us would be able to crack. Would you have any idea about codes he used?"

"No. I don't recall him ever using codes."

"Do you have access to his safe?"

"Safe***s***, actually. I have one here. There are two up in his study. I have access to the one here and the visible one in his study. The one behind the picture was his private place. I don't even know where he might have kept the combination. Wait. There is an envelope in first safe in his den. It's one of those 'open only in case of my death' deals. It sits at the bottom since it's never been needed. His attorney may have something also, though Adam really never trusted anybody else with anything. I imagine combinations and codes are all here someplace."

"I will want to look into the contents of both safes as soon as possible. Are there just the three in the house?"

"No. Dorothy has one in her room. It was burglarized a few months ago and much of her jewelry was taken."

"How did the burglar gain entry?"

"Dorothy never locked it. She's not good with combinations. She would close it but not flip the handle into the lock position. That way she could just pull it open. It appeared to be locked unless you knew which position the handle was supposed to be in."

"Was the person caught?"

"No."

"How did he gain access to the house?"

"Probably walked right in through the front door. It's never locked except at night. This lower area off the entry hall is the business area. The door needs to be open so people can come and go. The robbery happened sometime between ten and ten thirty on a Wednesday morning. That's coffee break hour around here. We all gather in the kitchen and drink coffee and get fat on Millie's goodies."

"And just who is it that gathers?"

"Dotty, Raggs, Millie and me. Sometimes Alex drops in but not always."

"Guy?"

"No, Guy is pretty much the loner. I've seen him in the kitchen late at night sometimes with Dotty. She's about the only one he seems comfortable with."

"On the day of the robbery was Alex with you for coffee?"

"Yes he was. The only reason I remember is that the police asked the same question at the time."

"Do you think that robbery could have been an inside job - someone from the household? Masters asked."

"Maybe, though I doubt it. Like I said, everybody but Guy was in the kitchen. He was off getting some supplies at the hardware. During the investigation the clerks there vouched for him – day, time and so on."

"Adam?"

"Out of town - San Francisco. Gone all week."

"Back to Adam's death. Any chance it was John Haven?"

"About as much chance as the sun won't come up tomorrow. Not that he didn't have lots of reasons to want Adam dead but you have to know John. He's the stereotypic myopic bookkeeper. He handled the finances once they were in the company hands. Paid bills, made deposits, funded investments, payroll, anything that had to do with the company's money. He had a keen sense for investing. I'd guess about half the profits actually came from his investments rather than sales."

"Why did Adam fire him?"

"Well, *fire him* isn't exactly correct. John was a silent partner - had a ten or fifteen percent interest in the company. Adam had the rest so John served the company as vice president at Adam's pleasure, you might say. He still has his share in the company - just not the position. It seemed like a pretty good deal to me. No work to do. No Adam to put up with. And he still gets his same share of the profits as usual. It's a deal I'd take, I'll tell you that."

"Still, if he was so valuable to the business, why demote him, so to speak? Why force him to stop doing what he seemed to do so well?"

"It's a mystery to me. Adam wasn't given to whims. He would have had good reason. Maybe John is the one who Adam thought was threatening him. I don't know. I do know John couldn't have masterminded the chandelier thing. He has trouble fitting a key into his car's ignition. Not the handy type."

"If he were in on it, would you have any candidates for an accomplice?"

"He and Alex were always close. Sometimes he and Guy would smoke cigars in the gazebo out back. No real association with either Millie or Raggs. I'm rambling because I really have no idea how to answer your question."

"And you. What did *you* have to gain from his death?"

"Well, I lost my monthly "fee" like all his other ex-girls, but I'm in his will for enough to retire on - if I'm careful about my lifestyle. I'll probably lose my job in the long run. Dorothy wants to sell the business as soon as she can."

"Dorothy is the main beneficiary, then?"

"Sort of. She gets control of Adam's liquid assets in the company but none of his investments or property. It's rather hard to explain. She's also the beneficiary of a life insurance policy in the millions."

"What about those things she doesn't get? Who gets them?"

"Strange as it may seem, Alexander!"

"And he is aware of that?"

"I'm really not sure. Thing is, he won't want it - probably will try to refuse it. That may be why Adam left it to him - all the complicated aspects of an inheritance. It'll take years to untangle all of it. I can see Adam laughing his rear end off at the very thought of forcing Alex's involvement that way."

"Are the other employees remembered in the will?"

"Yes, all pretty much equally and quite generously, actually. Probably to make them feel guilty about how they felt about him all those years."

"You certainly paint a picture of an uncharitable man with no redeeming qualities."

"Good. Then I have been successful in describing him to you."

"Well, I appreciate your time. When will it be convenient for Detective Killroy and me to begin going through the safes? I expect him to return any time now."

"You just come and go as you please. It looks like I'll be here early 'til late for the next several weeks."

"By the way, would you contact the attorney and inquire about the combination to the third safe?"

"Right away."

Masters left, stopping briefly in the huge entry hall to plan his next move. Killroy entered and strode briskly toward him extending a large, brown envelope bearing the brutality of repeated recycling.

"Got some preliminaries on the crime scene," he announced as if it had all been due to his personal effort.

Masters' question, "What have you found?" was met with silence which tended to contradict the detective's initial presentation. Masters opened the envelope and removed half a dozen, ill-matched, sheets, clearly from various departments.

The blood on the Chandelier matched Adam's [Now *there's* a surprise!]. The top fingerprints (over-prints) on the chandelier bulbs and on its other surfaces belonged to Raggs, as would be expected. There were no prints on the central pipe in the area which had fit up into the collar in the attic - outside or inside.

The attic area was also clean. The only prints found up there were on the odd bulb over the opening. They did not belong to anyone in the household and the report noted their small size - most likely those of a child or petite woman. Most of the prints were smudged as would be expected from the very process of screwing in a bulb.

"Finally something to use," Masters said in response to that.

He made a note on the bottom of the page and handed it to Killroy.

"Make sure they run the prints from the attic bulb through the local files and the *Kid Safe* program in the schools."

"Yes, Sir. I'll sure see to that."

Neither end of the brass pipe that led through the back wall bore any prints. Master made another note and handed a second sheet to Killroy.

"We need to have the pipe that was inserted between the stones in the back wall, carefully removed by an expert so we can print its entire surface."

Killroy nodded and put the sheets into his inside coat pocket.

The wire was run of the mill, multi-strand, steel picture wire available in hundreds of local outlets. The wooden handle was a length of five eights inch dowel - the kind Alex had shown Masters earlier. Masters had also noticed several lengths on Guy's work shop area in his room. Again, it was a product available at hundreds of lumber and arts and craft outlets.

The stick attached to the other end of the wire – the one

that appeared to have been inserted into the hole in the collar - was pine, most likely cut from some standard one-by board. According to the report it had been inserted into that west hole, oriented in such a way that the weight of the chandelier rested on its weakest axis - with the grain running horizontally. The splinters on the collar and on the hole in the chandelier were a match insofar as they were all pine. The hole on the other end of the stick, through which the wire was secured, was drilled *with* the grain and not *across* or through the grain. That bothered Masters and deserved a line in his own notebook.

The identifiable prints on the desk in the study included Adam's, Betty's, Millie's, and Alex's. Several sets of unknowns were found at those places where a desk would typically be lifted and Masters assumed they would be found to match those of the carpet cleaning crew. The interesting fact was that each of the later sets of prints appeared in *three* slightly different places on the underside of the desk top. He jotted another note at the bottom of that sheet.

“I find nothing here about the code,” Masters said, peeking inside the envelope to make sure he hadn’t missed it.

“So far the computer is just spitting out gibberish. They emailed it to a cytologist in New York.”

Cytologist. It deserved and got a single snort from Masters.

"We need to find the workers who cleaned the carpet last. Betty can probably point you in their direction. I’d like for you to handle that personally, Detective."

Killroy swelled with importance. Masters smiled inside knowing it was a no-brainer and would keep the man occupied elsewhere for some time.

"Your people do good work, Detective. I need to go through the contents of the safes and I want you to be present to help verify the inventory. Do you have time for that now?"

"Yes, Sir. Taking inventory is one of my best things."

They entered Betty's office.

"Can you help us gain access to the safe in the study?" Masters asked.

"Sure. You want the combination or do you want me to come and open it?"

"I would prefer that you open it if you wouldn't mind. And a yellow pad if one is available."

"No problem. Right here."

Killroy proudly took custody of the pad.

The safe was soon open.

"Betty, if you'd just take a quick look inside to see if anything strikes you as odd – anything extra, missing, out of its usual place."

She looked. "No. Nothing seems strange. Adam was into it lots more than me so I'm not sure what to look for."

"That's fine. Thanks for your help. We'll call if we have questions."

The safe was less than modern. The inside compartment was an eighteen inch cube with a variety of cubicles and a small strong box sitting on the bottom.

"Do you know where the key to the steel box might be?" Masters called to Betty as she approached the door to leave.

"Top right drawer of his desk. Pull up on the front wooden divider. There is a slot in the bottom that holds it."

She waited to make sure it was located before leaving. Masters held it up for her to see and nodded his thanks.

"So where do we start?" Killroy asked, pad at the ready.

"How about the box?"

It contained little of interest - several thousand dollars in bills, a ring of what appeared to be spare house and car keys, several bearer bonds and Adam's passport. On the bottom, face down, was the envelope Betty had referred to. Inside it was an index card that caught Masters' attention. Hand printed at the top was an equation:

B / 1 = 6 / 2

Across the center were a series of five numbers separated by dashes. 10 - 41 - 33 - 18 - 28. He copied it into his pad exactly as it appeared.

"The string of numbers could be a combination - maybe to the other safe. I don't have a clue about the equation but it's bound to be relevant in some way."

Killroy looked about.

"The other safe?" He asked.

"Betty says there is a second safe in here behind a picture. Let's see where it is."

They began looking. Killroy found it behind and to the East of the desk.

"Try the combination," Masters suggested.

"That presents a problem," Killroy said, scratching his head.

"What's that?"

"The tumbler system on this safe is manufactured for a four number combination."

Masters apparently looked surprised.

"I've studied safes," Killroy explained. "Got interested when they had the robbery here a couple of months ago. Mrs. Williams' safe is just like this one – fireproof, holds about one cubic foot, and is recessed into the wall. But they don't have five numbers in their combinations, I can tell you that."

"I assume the combinations can be changed by the owner." Masters asked.

"Yes. Fairly simply, in fact. There's a plate on the inside of the door behind the tumbler that can be removed and it opens into an area where that can be done by turning a set of dials. Even so, the combination has to remain four numbers."

"Well, Adam clearly put an extra set of numbers in the series on this card to foil anyone who found it. No immediate way of knowing which set it is. In fact, from what I have learned about Adam, we can't even be sure what order is going to prove to be the correct one. I imagine the equation at the top provides the necessary clue. I will work on that later. Let's just let that one be for now."

Killroy agreed, clearly pleased that he had made a real contribution.

During the next half hour dozens of documents were inventoried - all business related and none of apparent relevance to the murder. There was a list of females' names, ad-

addresses and phone numbers and a ledger which showed regular payments to those same people. Masters supposed they were Adam's 'women' and the entries represented the 'consultation fees' they were paid each month. Betty was called to verify that. His hunch had been correct.

"Well, that pretty well wraps it up here until we find a way into that other safe."

"We can have the boys drill it open. It'll take a while but we can get it open," Killroy suggested.

"We may have to resort to that. I'd rather crack the combination because it may provide a lead to the other code Adam used."

"I see. Well, okay then. Would this be a good time for me to get onto the carpet cleaner side of our case?"

"Yes. That's probably the next really important part of all this."

Masters closed and locked the safe and the two left the study. At the bottom of the stairs Killroy left through the front door and Masters circled back toward his room. Betty called to him.

"I contacted the attorney and he has no codes or safe combinations. Sorry."

Masters nodded. Once in his room he arranged several things on the desk - the coded sheet from Adam's folder, his copies of the death threats provided by Millie, the index card from the safe and a fresh new yellow pad.

Masters muttered to himself. "B over 1 = 6 over 2 . The simple algebraic solution to that would be that B equals 3. It seems too simple but perhaps that was the intent - to make the obvious seem incorrect. B! B! Why not X? What could B stand for? Perhaps the old safe was safe A and the new one was Safe B - but that moves me no closer to a solution to the combination and if the equation is to be a clue, then it has to represent something else."

He stood and paced. He got a drink of water. Alex was right – it reeked of chlorine. He removed his sweater. He sat in the large upholstered chair beside the window and closed his eyes. Presently, they popped open.

"B is for *beginning* - the beginning of the actual combination. He couldn't have used S for *start* because S could have also meant second. He couldn't have used F for *first* because that could have also meant fourth or fifth. It made perfect sense that B = 3 meant that the first two numbers - 10 and 41 - were to be skipped and that the combination **B**egan with the third number. A simple solution to a potentially complicated process. It made the combination: 33 - 18 - 28 - and then back to the first one, 10.

He dialed 67 on the phone and soon he and Raggs were in the study. Masters wouldn't open it without a witness present. He walked directly to the safe and began turning the dial. It opened on the first try.

Inside were two large envelopes. One had miscellaneous business papers, lists of names and addresses, and several deeds in it - not of immediate interest to Masters. The second contained a manila filing folder. Under the envelopes, on the bottom of the safe, wrapped in a piece of black satin was an old pistol. The men carefully deposited it in an evidence bag and continued their search.

Inside the manila file folder were the three postcards, which Millie had described, and a single sheet of paper.

Masters examined the sheet. It contained another coded message. It was on a plain white, 8 1/2 by 11 piece of second sheet stationary. Different from the other message in that *it* had been written less formally on the back of a smaller page torn from a phone message pad provided as advertising from a box company.

"Another message," Masters said, showing it to Raggs

"A *long* message the way it looks," Raggs said.

"Are you into Codes and such - cryptograms?" Masters asked.

"I dabble."

"Dabble?" The term just seemed amusing coming from Raggs' refined lips.

"Yes. I got into it through the back door, you might say.

Millie and Mr. Williams have - had - a decade long *Cryptowar* going on between them. They would see who could solve the daily cryptograms first each morning. I'd watch for the buttons on the phone to light up and must admit I would listen in to see who had won. I stayed in the background, doing them myself - like a silent participant if there can be such a thing. Occasionally I would beat them both and treat myself to a cup of sherbet. I'd say that Millie was first six times out of ten.

"It was an inane competition but good for more laughs than you can imagine. Though neither would admit it, they both took it very seriously. When Millie won, Mr. W. would stomp around for hours. When Mr. W. won Millie would bang the poor pots and pans unmercifully 'til lunch. It was one of those wonderful little pleasures in my life, which I shall sorely miss. This, however, does not appear to be a simple substitution cryptogram."

"What leads you to that conclusion so quickly?" Masters asked, intrigued at the man's apparent prowess.

"Well first of all, of course, it is composed of digits rather than letters but that would not necessarily rule out some sort of one to one substitution system. But see here, there are four twos in a row. No English word has four of any one letter in a row - nor does German, Erse, French, Italian or Spanish for that matter."

"A linguist as well?"

"As you are aware, I was raised in England. The study of languages is always a required part of education there. It's a good thing I believe. With each new language you gain the capacity to think in slightly different ways. That allows useful perspectives." He broke into a confidential whisper: "Why, we even learned to speak *American*."

He chuckled out loud. Masters followed his lead, more at the humor in Raggs enjoying his own little joke, than at the joke itself.

"If this is not a simple substitution code - and I agree that it isn't - do you have any ideas about it?" Masters asked.

"Not a clue!" came his quick and definite response.

"Well, I'll make a copy and then dispatch it to Killroy's cryptographers.

Masters patted his expansive mid-section.

"Suppose Millie might have some delectable something to sustain an old man 'til dinner?"

"I'm sure of it," Raggs answered and the two were off in search of treats like little boys heading for the candy store."

CHAPTER FOUR
Day one: The Evening

"Well, I thought you two was going to stand me up this afternoon," were Millie's opening remarks as Raggs and Masters entered the kitchen. "Coffee's fresh and so are the Apricot Swirls."

"Sounds scrumptious," Master said as the two took seats opposite each other at the timeworn little table. "Any luck with the code, yet," Masters inquired.

" 'Fraid not. It's beyond my old brain."

"It seems to be beyond the old computer at the forensics lab, too, so I suppose that puts you in pretty good company."

Masters reached for a paper napkin and with his pen begin sketching the stick found attached to the wire in the attic. He spoke to Raggs as he worked.

"Just listen and tell me if I'm missing something."

Raggs nodded, his interest piqued.

"What we found in the attic - the wire, the handle hanging down outside by guy's window and the stick that fit the hole in the collar - appears to be the method by which the chandelier was released so it would come crashing down on Adam. It was made to appear as though the stick was a simple replacement for the iron rod that went through the holes holding the fixture securely in place – otherwise it would not have been made a foot long. We are to believe that at some point, someone reached out guy's window, pulled the wire by using the wooden handle, the stick was pulled free through the holes and the chandelier released. Does that seem to be the set-up?"

"Yes, that's how it is supposed to appear."

Masters continued.

"But, the weight of the chandelier would exert far too much pressure – weight – on the stick to allow it to be slipped out of the holes with a simple tug on the wire – even if it were pulled straight out, let alone at an angle. Plus, the composition of the stick is far too weak to support that weight in the first place. Now, look here at this sketch. The way the stick has sloughed off at the end tells us it would have been slid into the hole so the grain ran crossways, the weak way – it came apart in layers. That suggests some knowledge of how much weight the stick could hold in each axis, I imagine - that's not clear but let me go on. Now, look at the hole in the other end through which the wire was strung and tied. It was bored *with* the grain – through just a single layer, so to speak - rather than across the grain and down through several layers. One good tug and the wire would have cut its way out the end of the stick. Had it been bored against the grain, it would have been much stronger. The question is, why would someone who knew exactly how to position the support end, make such an elementary error when boring the hole in the other end?"

"I see your point. The designer never intended to have it pulled out by the wire - and yes, your characterization all seems correct to me."

"The conclusion has to be then . . ."

"That the entire wire arrangement is a sham, a distracter, a false lead never intended to be used," Raggs added, finishing the statement for Masters, with his characteristic precision.

"And yet the wood splinters on the chandelier and the metal collar do seem to have come from that stick with the crumpled end that we both just agreed could not have been used in the manner that someone so carefully laid out."

"It's as if - if I may, Sir" - Raggs began, "Someone with minimal know-how was trying to frame Guy."

The treats and coffee arrived. Millie, kibitzing from across the room, had her own two cents worth to add.

"Guy is not the smartest cookie on the plate, but he is definitely smart enough not to leave the incriminating evidence dangling outside his own window."

"Not unless," Masters went on, "He wanted it to be found."

"Why would he want it to be found?" she asked, clearly puzzled.

"To make us think exactly what we do think - that he was too smart to have incriminated himself that way. It's like if *you* had killed the man, Millie, you might have put arsenic in his oatmeal. Everybody would know that you are too smart to have done it in a way that so obviously incriminated yourself, so you would move way down on the suspect list. It would seem that someone was trying to set you up."

"Crime fighting is certainly a complicated affair," Millie said.

"My Dear, you just keep to making Apricot Swirls and I'll take care of the crime fighting," came Masters' smiling response.

"That's a deal, Mr. M. Well, maybe."

Masters and Raggs looked at one another, questions on their faces. Millie explained.

"The dial on the oven busted in two and I've glued it so often it won't hold together no more. I gotta use the pliers and just guess where to set the temperature 'til I get somebody in here to replace it. Until then, the future of goodies are up for grabs."

"May I be of assistance with that?" Raggs asked

"I hope so. I got the phone number of the repair man but he's got so fancy on his new business card I've had all kinds of trouble reaching him."

"Fancy?" Raggs asked.

Millie took the card from the shelf beside the wall phone

and handed it to Raggs.

"God intended that phone *numbers* should be _numbers_," she went on dramatically. "He got fancy and made his into words - see it says for emergencies simply dial o-v-e-n-f-i-x. I can't never read those tiny little letters on the phone buttons. 'Bout the time I'm finally getting close to the end, the operator's voice comes on saying if I want to make a call I should hang up and dial again. I've come to hate that sickeningly sweet voice. If you wouldn't mind making the call, I'd sure be beholdin' to you."

"I'll see to it at once."

Master's face lit up. He stood and planted the kiss of all kisses on Millie's cheek.

"You and your broken oven may have just solved one important part of this thing, Miss Mill. Excuse me."

He hurried [well!] back to his room and was soon busy at the desk. As was his penchant, he mumbled to himself as he worked.

"I knew that a man like Adam would leave us a clue to the code. After all, he did want it deciphered or he wouldn't have written it. And, anyway, he was about to tell us its contents at the moment he died. Totally out of character, he wrote the message on the back of a phone message page. *That* was his clue! I should have seen it earlier - the code is related to the number and letter buttons on the phone. Each number button also represents several letters. I'll list the numbers from his message and then place all the possible letters under them. Let's see where that leads us."

4.	5	3	7	8	3	7	5	4	5	5	3	3	4	4	7
G	J	D	P	T	D	P	J	G	J	J	D	D	G	G	P
H	K	E	Q	U	E	Q	K	H	K	K	E	E	H	H	Q
I	L	F	R	V	F	R	L	I	L	L	F	F	I	I	R
			S			S									S

6	3	7	4	3	9	'7	3	2	8	4	3	7	- 2	7	9
M	D	P	G	D	W	P	D	A	T	G	D	P	A	P	W
N	E	Q	H	E	X	Q	E	B	U	H	E	Q	B	Q	X
O	F	R	I	F	Y	R	F	C	V	I	F	R	C	R	Y
		S			Z	S						S		S	Z

"Now, let's see what we can make out of this jumble. I'm betting that one of the three or four possible letters in each set when combined with the correct ones from the other sets will make words. No wonder the computer blew its chips!

"The first number is 4 and it represents a stand alone letter so you'd think it would be either A or I. From number button 4 it could not be A, just I. But with the period after it I wonder if it may not be an initial instead. Let's move on.

"I'll jump over to the fourth word. Only three letters so it should be a good place to begin. There is only one possible vowel choice - I - probably in the middle looking at the odd letter choices. Let's see: gip, giq, gir, gis, hip, hiq, hir, his - HIS the last choice but finally a useful word. I'll go with that. Let's look at the final three letter word. It can contain no vowels - well, there is the Y so we could have the word CRY. My feeling is that word would not fit into his kind of a message but it might. If not, those three letters could be some kind of abbreviation. The hyphen before them makes me wonder. I often put a hyphen before my initials on short notes. Could it be? The A and W could certainly stand for Adam Williams. I guess I don't know his middle name."

A quick call to Betty revealed it was Paul and there, right where it needed to be was the P.

"I'll go with that as being his signature initials. Let's go back to the second word - only two vowels and both E's. Can probably rule out a word ending in EQ or EP. That leaves ER or ES - both good possibilities."

He sat back and just let his eyes roam over the block of letters. It jumped out at him LESTER.

"That means the first stand alone letter is probably not "I" but Lester's first initial – "G."

"Let's attack the word with the apostrophe. The period was intended to be a period. Therefore, I'll assume the apostrophe is, in fact, an apostrophe. That would make the final letter a T or an S. The only choice will be S and that means a possessive rather than a contraction. Someone's name, I assume. Let's see. The only player I am aware of whose name begins with one of those letters - M, N, O - Is Millie and clearly her name cannot be spelled with the remaining choices. I guess I need her last name."

Another call was placed to Betty. Millie Mitchell.

"Well, Mitchell doesn't fit either. Another route, then. Not a name. Hummm. Again only E's for the two possible vowels. The 7 and 4 could be the SH combination but that doesn't really work with the possibilities in front of it. Those could also be PH. Same problem. Hummm. NO! wait. NEPH *could* be a winner. And follow that with the given E. The only choice left would be W as in nephew's. OK Raymond! Break out the sherbet!! Let's see we have, 'G. LESTER *blank* HIS NEPHEW'S *blank* – APW'.

"The third word has six letters and again only two vowels are available so both will probably be used. That makes it __ I __ __ E __. Only two of the three last letter choices are possibles, ED or EF - unlikely it would be EE. ED would be the more common choice. If the middle letters are double letters, they would have to be L's, and since I doubt if Adam was concerned about being 'Jilled' or 'Lilled' the word is logically *KILLED*. So that makes it, G. LESTER KILLED HIS NEPHEW'S blank. And there it is! G. LESTER KILLED HIS NEPHEW'S FATHER - APW. That APW probably is not a signature as I first assumed but the obviating definition of the word 'father'. He wanted there to be no doubt that he had reason to believe Guy was trying to kill him - APW. Why not just come out and say that, especially in a coded message? Probably because Adam wanted us to know that he knew about Guy's relation to Alex's natural father and to Alex – uncle and nephew. At the announcement meeting he not only intended to implicate Guy (who, interestingly, suspiciously even, had not been invited) but also blow Alex's world apart with the fatherhood revelation. Was that just because he was such a contemptible human being or because he had some other motive – perhaps indicating a possible second suspect – if not Guy, then Alex?

"The evidence tends to support Adam's conclusion – there

being no one else with even a shred of evidence pointing in their direction. Problem: Guy was on the roof working alone. We need to find witnesses that saw him there. Quite unlikely I'm afraid, but look on the bright side. It's another job to occupy Detective Killroy.

"Even more of a problem: I have no real evidence as to how the chandelier drop was actually triggered. The rope and bow knot has possibilities but it requires someone's presence in the attic at the moment of release and then in someway that person had to be able to leave clandestinely with the rope immediately after the incident. That is a possibility of course since confusion reigned for several minutes and everyone in the house was almost immediately congregated in the study.

"I have to wonder what Adam's evidence against Guy was - is. And why he didn't present it? Perhaps it's all another game - his last - telling who it is but making *us* prove it. Perhaps all he had was supposition but having been born from his huge ego I'm sure that was all he felt was necessary. There is still a major part of the puzzle missing. Perhaps the other coded message from his private safe will help."

Before he could begin working on it, there was a knock on his door. It was Killroy - ever smiling Detective K. Roy Killroy, A.S.S.

"Come in. Hope you have something useful. All I have here are dead ends."

"Well, I'm afraid I have another one to add to your list. The *Fresh Way Carpet Cleaners* have a sign on their door saying they are closed for two weeks to attend the wedding of the owner's sister in Italy. I asked around the neighborhood but nobody seems to know much about them except they are all short, dark complected, and speak Italian most of the time. It just might be that they are foreigners."

This time it *had* to be an attempt at humor. No human being, loose on the street, could actually be that stupid. Masters chuckled. Killroy laughed well beyond what was called for, prolonging his little joke for as long as possible.

"I'll go back and check out the owner's home address if

you want. Maybe somebody around there knows a place to call in Italy."

"That's a good idea, Detective. In the mean time I need your help on another matter."

Killroy produced his pad, ready for the details.

"See if you can find anyone in the neighborhood who saw Guy working on the roof at the time of the murder – about 9:02 AM this morning. I imagine it's just a knock on doors kind of job."

"I'm on it."

He turned to leave.

"I'll walk you to the door" Masters said. "I need to locate Raggs and Millie."

Raggs was dusting vases, which were perched on Greek looking pedestals in the entry hall.

"Feather dusting is an exercise in futility," he said to Masters as if presenting some important lesson about life.

"The dust is whisked into the air and as soon as I move on to the next, it resettles back to where it had been comfortable in the first place. Much like a married man's mid-life affair with a younger woman, I suppose."

"And then why is it that you continue to feather dust?"

"It is in the *List of Duties* and a good butler never veers from his *List of Duties*."

"Yours is not to question why . . . ?"

"Precisely. May I help you?"

"For the record I'm listing the whereabouts of all the household members at the moment of Adam's death."

"Well, not having been in the study, I'm not sure when that occurred, precisely. I would have been somewhere between five and fifteen meters down the hall toward Alex's studio."

"You pull my leg so well, Raggs."

"I do my best, Sir."

He smiled his rare – though recently more frequent - smile.

"Actually, I had just entered the hall from the study when

when Mr. Williams topped the stairs and walked toward me. I opened the door for him, closed it after him, and spent a few seconds contemplating the top, right hinge. I thought I detected the faintest squeak. I made a mental note to mention it to Guy and then moved on toward Alex's studio. I try to keep things straightened up in there but the young man dislikes having me around when he is working so I was going to take advantage of his absence. I had just reached the studio door when I heard the crash and the women screaming. I turned around and made straight away back into the study."

"The record thanks you, Raggs. Any Idea where Millie was?"

"Well, yes I do. I feel like a boy telling tales out of school, however."

Masters gave him a blank look.

"I'm sure she'll tell you the same. She was following Mr. Williams up the stairs - probably a dozen steps behind, carrying fresh linens. She turned and headed toward Guy's room with them. I can't say I saw her enter his room but there's nothing else down there."

"Thank you and I am sure she *will* verify that, herself. You were reluctant because . . .?"

"Because my story places her within easy access of the window and the wire."

"But we have determined that could not have been the instrument of the murder, haven't we."

"Yes, I know, but it also puts her in the room where the steps lead to the attic and perhaps to a bow knot just needing a simple tug."

"I see. You have been thinking, haven't you?

"Always. Most of Butlering is mindless monotony. It gives me an abundance of time to contemplate this and that."

"Well, I'll leave you to your dust and reflections on the male, mid-life crisis."

Masters made his way to the kitchen. Millie was not in sight but he heard her belting out, *"Are Ye Able,"* in the distance. There was a door at the far end of the kitchen. Masters approached. It was ajar so he pressed it open. It was the laundry.

"Hey, Mr. M. Got dirty duds for me?" came Millie's cheery greeting.

"Probably, but that's not my immediate mission."

She continued folding and sorting the freshly dried clothes into six, brightly colored plastic baskets – apparently one for each member of the household.

"I'm just finishing the official record of where everybody was in the house at the moment of the murder and you are my last entry."

Her answer came without hesitation or thought.

"I was in the kitchen, setting up the dough for those Apricot Swirls. They don't make themselves you know. Twice raised dough. It don't pay to try and do it in one. They just lay there lifeless on the plate, you know. No spring in the chew."

It was too much prattle even for Millie and not the information Masters was expecting. A new dilemma. Either Raggs or Millie was not being truthful. If it were Raggs he was trying to implicate Millie. Why? To cover for himself? Someone else? Who? If it were Millie, she was trying to place herself somewhere other than in the vicinity of Guy's room at the time of the death. Why? Most obviously, to protect herself?"

It had been an unexpected turn of events and Masters thought it best not to press the discrepancy at that moment.

"Well, thanks for your help," he said turning to leave.

"Dinner at seven, remember," she called after him. "Informal except Sundays then everybody gets all gussied up - well everybody but Alex. It's the one meal a week he never misses. I think he comes just so he can antagonize the others by arriving in his grubbies. He's a handsome specimen when he does get dressed up though, I'll tell you that."

Millie clearly loved Alex and that would be natural - it appeared to have been her, more than anyone else, who had raised him. Masters looked at his watch. It was five fifteen.

"Just the right amount of time before dinner for a short

snack," he said aloud as he passed the one remaining Apricot Swirl on his return trip through the kitchen.

He snatched it from the plate. That, of course necessitated a mug of coffee – always available there, he was learning. A few minutes later he was back in his room sitting at the desk enjoying Millie's culinary handiwork.

He removed the second coded message from its folder and returned to his muttering. For Masters, muttering was not muttering in the sense that it indicated he was either old or grumpy. It was merely a time tested method to enhance his capacity to think. He would describe it as a way to approach his brain simultaneously from the inside and the outside.

"This message, having been in his private safe, makes me believe that Adam must have regarded it as extremely valuable or even, perhaps, as something to be guarded from prying eyes until after his death."

Masters stroked his mustache.

"Let's see what we have here. Actually it looks like two separate codes have been used. The short, twelve word, message in two sentences across the top appears to be a straight forward cryptogram - but then few things have been as they seemed so far. I'll approach it that way initially. The rest of it is sets of hyphenated numbers: 8-4, 1-7 and so on. They fill the rest of the page. Different from the other sheet, this one has been typed or key boarded or whatever it's called these days. Probably printed out on the laser printer in his study. Would that have been for neatness, clarity, precision, or perhaps just so it could all fit in an easily readable fashion on a single sheet. I'll go with that one for now. It is also different in that this document has Adam's full name signature plainly written at the bottom, dated four years ago, and notarized. It is far longer, also – looks to be about seventy-five words. An efficient man like Adam could say a great deal in seventy-five words."

Masters copied the first line onto a fresh sheet in his yellow pad.

ACX BDD, EYFDB, GJMD HIXKDB, OXBF PD XBDE HICHDIGA. XX JB K Y E Y.

"Where to begin?"

[Please feel free to work it out yourself before proceeding; Of course it may *not* be a straight forward cryptogram!]

"There are no stand alone letters this time. That second word is one of Millie's favorite sequences - inn, ill, see, fee, wee. That B also occurs at the end of two words where the S often sits so let's begin with SEE - I like the E option because in the code, D is the most frequent letter and that's often E. That makes the two letter word end in E which makes it BE or HE or ME or WE. The P – whatever it is - is not used elsewhere so it won't make any difference if I find that now or not. For grammatical purposes I'll just assume for the time being that it's the verb, BE.

"The first two words seem to represent a phrase being set off by the comma. What three letter word before SEE makes sense as part of a phrase - *NOW* SEE - probably not. *YOU* SEE - a good possibility. I'll go with that tentatively. That gets us at least one more frequently occurring letter - the U. Interesting because U is not typically a frequently occurring vowel in English. If it is U, it makes me think the eighth word is USED, which would make the third word begin with a D. D *blank blank* ES. The vowel there has to be either A or I since the others have been used. Try A. DAMES, DANES, DARES, DATES. The first two seem illogical for the note. If DATES, that makes F represent T which makes the sixth word end in UST - can't be bust if BE is correct. LUST is a possibility but that doesn't fit with the following word BE. MUST fits. Let's make the O represent M. What else does that do? Nothing.

"Looking at the last word ending in E *blank*, *blank*, Y. My guess would be LY so let's see what that does. It makes word four L *blank*, *blank*, E. It needs another vowel and I is all we have left. Typically, only vowels follow the letter L so it becomes LI *blank* E. LIVE, LIFE, LIKE, LICE, LIME, LINE. Can't be LIME - the M has been found. LIKE is the best bet since it and the following word are set off by commas, like some kind of phrase. Back to that last word. It ends in E *blank* LY. E*T*LY, E*N*LY and E*D*LY are unlikely. Could be E*R*LY. It puts two R's into that word so it would become *blank* RO *blank* ERLY *and* the two blanks are the same letter. Let's do it the easy way and just go through the alphabet. Not many consonants can precede an R. I'll bet on P and that makes the word PROPERLY. What's left? That fifth word then becomes PRUNES – unlikely but then . . . . All the letters making up the second sentence have already been found. So the translation is:

ACX BDD, EYFDB, GJMD HIXKDB
YOU SEE, DATES, LIKE PRUNES,

OXBF PD XBDE HICHDIGA.
MUST BE USED PROPERLY.

XX JB K Y E Y
UU IS NADA

"So I solve one puzzle and it presents me with another. Undoubtedly this is Adam's clue to decoding the main body of the message below. It was the method he used on the safe combination card."

Masters' large frame began jiggling as he chuckled to himself.

"That man had some interesting sense of humor, I'll say that much. *Dates, like prunes, must be used properly.*"

"*Dates* can mean fruit, entries on a calendar, or romantic outings - I suppose any kind of meeting, actually. *Prunes* can mean fruit or dried fruit and I guess stretching it a bit could mean a dislikable old person or some such being - could that be a reference to Adam, himself? The last four words - *Must be used properly* - seem to be offering some kind of caution or direction about the use of whatever kind of *date* it may be. Or maybe to highlight it as some unique application. Was the word *prune* added to define date as a fruit or, knowing Adam, to be some play on word or simply a distracter?

"That second section, *UU IS NADA*. *Nada* is Spanish for *nothing,* I believe. UU could mean a lot of things. Unitarian Univeralists - In that case quite a few of the Southern Baptists I know might agree that *UU is Nada*."

He chuckled again, more prolonged than probably necessary.

"UU? University of Utah. UU? Uncomfortable Underwear. UU? A *double* U. Perhaps that's it. *W is nothing.* It still makes no sense but perhaps it is a starting clue - he was giving us the code for W. That could be 0 or 0-0. Whatever it means, it is not clear to me."

"Adam certainly wanted these two simple lines to be a clue to help in opening the main, more ingeniously coded message. Why else would they have been included? If so, however, I would have expected it to be more straight forward than this. He must have had reason to keep even his clue, cryptic. It makes me believe the contents are in some way so important that he felt they needed to be painstakingly guarded. Perhaps Killroy's code guys will see something I don't. It may be some standard code form. It does look strange, however.

4-4 3-5 1-2 11-3 2-2 2-3 2-2 6-4 1-3 1-5
12-1 9-2 8-5 4-2 4-4 3-4 1-5 10-5 4-5 9-2
3-5 6-2 3-1 2-6 1-3 12-6 9-5 4-4 5-3 8-3.
4-4 12-1 4-4 12-1 11-1 ' 8-6
7-3 9-8 3-2 1-6 1-3 3-5 10-1 0-0 9-4 10-4
12-6 12-2 10-1 10-3 3-5 10-6 2-4 0-0 4-4 9-1 11-4 ,
1-3 10-4 2-7 12-1 4-4 12-1 4-4 8-6 3-3 1-7 .
4-4 0-0 1-2 5-3 9-4 11-7 12-1
12-1 10-1 4-3 10-4 10-3 3-5 2-8 5-1 10-1 9-9 2-2
2-5 6-4 10-2 1-5 7-2 8-5 9-2 4-4
12-3 10-4 6-2 4-5 12-1 11-1 ' 8-6
0-0 4-4 1-3 3-5 9-5 11-8 3-5 9-8 2-6 12-8 9-4
10-3 3-5 3-2 5-3 10-5 10-6 3-4 1-2 6-2 8-5 11-4
4-4 7-3 10-4 11-3 11-7 12-1 3-5 12 -2 1-6.

7-3 10-1 11-3 2-2 1-5 11-1 12-1 4-4
2-6 2-4 6-4
9-1 8-6 2-7 3-2 1-3 8-3 9-2 3-3 9-1.
0-0 4-4 5-3 11-1 4-4 1-3 8-3 2-6 11-1 12-1
4-4 1-5 11-8 12-1 7-5 10-1 11-3 9-8 12-8 8-5.
9-1 10-1 , 4-4 2-1 9-9 2-6 9-6 9-5 12-1
3-5 10-6 2-7 12-6 10-1 4-5 10-4 11-3 9-8 12-1
4-2 11-4 8-6 6-4 1-6 , 9-3 1-2 7-4 4-4 11-1 8-3
0-0 4-4 8-6 5-3 10-6 8-5 9-1 11-7 8-5 , 2-6 5-3 12-1
4-2 2-2 43 9-3 9-2 9-4 1-6 1-2 10-3 10-4 1-6 9-1
3-2 1-3 12-1 3-4 10-4 5-3 8-5 8-2 3-1 4-4 1-3 8-3
2-1 10-1 1-4 2-4
4-4 1-3 11-1 10-4 1-2 9-5 5-1 9-4
7-5 4-4 11-3 6-4 9-1 4-4 11-1 8-6 3-5 2-2
9-3 2-4 10-1 12-3 10-6 9-1 8-5. 10-3 3-5 9-5
12-8 2-2 10-02 10-1 2-7 12-1
9-1 3-5 10-4 7-2 7-3 12-1 1-5 11-7
8-5 6-4 10-3 8-5 10-3 1-6 1-5 4-4 8-3 3-5 9-4.
4-4 8-6' 9-1 2-6 4-5 2-4 4-4 8-3 3-5 9-4
8-6 10-4 12-1 10-4 9-4 3-5 2-6 10-3
1-3 10-4 0-0 2-3 9-2 3-4 1-5 7-2 8-5 10-6
0-0 4-4 9-4 3-5 10-1 6-2 10-3 8-6 3-5 4-4 9-1
12-1 10-1 10-2 7-2 3-1 2-2 11-1 10-3
4-4 3-5 3-2 12-1
12-3 10-4 11-5 12-5 4-4 8-6 10-3 6-4 12-1
9-4 3-5 10-6 4-2 12-2 12-8 2-1 9-2 10-2 8-6
3-4 2-4 4-4 11-5 2-2.

Just look at that sea of digits and hyphens. I assume the wide spaces represent spaces between words. I also assume that each set of hyphenated digits represents a letter. In the first line he has given us the two stand alone letter words – one should be A and the other I. The 4-4 pattern occurs so frequently that I am going to assume that represents 'I' since this was written by an exceedingly self-centered person who can be expected to have made many self references. That leaves the 1-5 for the letter 'A'. Of course I count sixty-three distinct digit combinations. There being only 26 letters in the English alphabet that pretty well rules out any simple one for one substitution code. The largest left hand number – left of the hyphen – is twelve and the largest to the right is nine. The smallest on both sides is one – except for the 0-0 which I will assume stands for W. Some way *that* is going to be significant. I just don't see it at this point. If 0-0 does represent W that means the reference for the code probably contains no W but that since his message required W's he had to supply it separately. Perhaps that's why the *Spanish*, 'nada' – to set that short phrase apart as quite separate in meaning from the first. I will put it aside and start again when I am fresh."

* * * * * *

Dinner had been delicious. It was nearly eight thirty when Masters approached Guy's door. Unlike the always open door at Alex's studio, guy's was always locked. After the knock, Masters heard the telltale clicks of the lock being turned.

"Mr. Masters. I didn't expect you this evening – sometime, just not this evening."

"If it is a bad time . . ."

"Oh, no. Come in. Have a seat."

The two men sat, Masters on the couch and Guy on a matching chair.

"I've spoken with Dorothy about you, so we can just assume I know about your family relationship to Alex."

"I see. Well that makes it all less complicated, doesn't it? What can I do for you?"

"Any ides about Mr. Williams' killer?"

"Lots of ideas. Nothing solid. I'm sure nothing you haven't already heard. Everybody hated him. Everybody's happy now. I wish you could just let it go."

"That seems to be a popular viewpoint. I'm, really here about the jewel robbery several months ago. What can you tell me about it?"

"Not sure. A fireproof wall safe. Dotty never locked it – we all knew that. It was like a staff joke – 'Secure as something in Dotty's safe'."

"Did the staff know she kept her jewelry in it?"

"I'm not sure. Probably. I assumed she did. We never

spoke of it, really."

"That's all that was taken, I hear."

"That's what I hear, too. I'm afraid that I ain't gonna be much help."

"Did anybody seem particularly interested in its contents – what was taken – what was left behind?"

"That detective – the one with you earlier in the day. But that was his job, I suppose."

"Anything else that might have seemed strange or inappropriate at or around the time of the robbery? Anything may help," Masters urged.

"Well, maybe. A few hours after the detectives left, I was passing in the hall in front of Dotty's door. Alex came storming out of it cursing and tossing his hands in the air. I knocked, wanting to see if Dotty needed anything. When she didn't answer, I let myself in. She wasn't there – well, I figured she was in the bathroom. It all just seemed strange."

"Had you witnessed Alex and his mother having heated exchanges before?"

"Arguments? No. Never. Not between them. Well, maybe a few when he was a teenager but that was just his age."

"Are you close to Alex?"

"In some ways. We play chess Sunday evenings. It's been our time since he was about ten. Neither of us are much good. It's more just an excuse to be together I guess. He missed being with his father – a man in his life, I mean. I was his substitute, I suppose. It's been my honor, of course. I'm sure I could have done better than I have."

"Anything strange around here the past several months – new people coming and going, routine changes, temperament changes, anything at all?"

"Well yes, actually. Two things come to mind. I ain't discussed them with nobody. About six weeks ago I started getting a envelope in the mail every Monday morning. It always contains the same thing – five, one hundred dollar bills. I can't explain it. I've racked my brain."

"You said *two* things."

"Yes, well a lot of things seemed to take place all about that same time – six or eight weeks ago. About then, my box of private papers was rummaged through by someone. Nothing was taken but they was out of order and I knew somebody'd been into them. It's just an old cigar box – I don't have much that's worth keeping. My legal papers are in Dorothy's safe – it's fireproof and she offered to keep them years ago."

"What kind of papers are in the safe, if I may ask?"

"The usual things; social security card, birth certificate, the legal papers changing my name, some tax papers. Things like that."

"And here?"

Guy took the box from the drawer and began going through it, offering a few items for Masters to view.

"A couple of unusual baseball cards, special letters, prescriptions, address book, a few warranties for expensive things like the TV, and this picture of Peter and me with my parents when we were teenagers."

"But nothing was taken?" Masters asked as he held his hand out to receive the picture.

"No."

"My goodness, Guy, you and Peter could have been twins. I've never seen brothers that resembled one another so much. How much difference is in there your age?"

"I was eleven months younger to the day. I can't remember a time as a kid that I wasn't just as tall as Pete. He hated that! Sometimes strangers mistook me for the older one. I'd rub it in and he'd pound on me. He was always stronger."

"Was your box rifled before or after the jewel robbery?"

Guy took time to think.

"After. Right after, in fact."

"Who knew about your box?"

"I can't say for sure that anybody did. Sometimes Raggs straightens things up in here for me. He might have run across it, I suppose. Millie brings my laundry – I keep the box in the bottom drawer of my clothes chest – well you saw. Alex used to roam around in here. He liked to use my tools. He's always had free run of my place, I guess."

"I've noticed you keep your door locked. How would someone have gained entrance?"

"I just started locking the place since the incident with my box. May I ask you something?"

The question seemed ill timed in terms of the flow of the conversation. Masters could not resist.

"Certainly. I imagine you want to know the secret of my diet, don't you?"

It drew an actual smile, but no comment.

"I'm just wondering if Alex is a suspect in the murder."

"As much as anyone else at this point, I guess. He was in the study when it happened. That's a pretty good alibi, though, I'd say."

"That leaves just Millie, Raggs and me without good alibis then, I guess. What if nobody had an alibi? Would Alex be high on your list, then?"

It was an odd but clearly serious and very interesting question. Masters gave a noncommittal response.

"I hadn't thought about it from that perspective, I guess, so it's hard to say. Well, I've kept you long enough. Thanks for your help."

Guy saw him to the door and shut it behind him.

'Click, click.'

Masters smiled.

As Masters descended the stairs he met Betty just leaving for the day.

"You keep long hours," he said, attempting to strike up a conversation.

"It seems I could say the same for you."

"May I bend your ear for just two more minutes?"

"Sure. What's on your mind?"

"Thinking back - say two months - have you noticed any special change in any member of the household?"

"Change? Well, I'm not sure what you're looking for. Guy started locking his door. Dotty began locking her safe.

Raggs changed his day off from Monday to Thursday. Alex is always so unpredictable I'm not sure I'd even notice if he had changed in any way. Well, yes, in fact. Alex. He's always called Adam 'Pops'. It enraged the man but he hid it well. Alex knew how it affected him, of course. It was part of their on-going battle. Alex would discover new ways to hassle his father and Adam would valiantly make it appear that he remained unruffled by it all.

"But about two months ago – give or take ten days or so - Alex began calling his father *Adam* - a very crisp, clipped, Adam. I figure it was another way he thought he could infuriate the man – though I guess thinking about it I'm not sure how it would have accomplished that. I don't think of anything else. Millie still sings hymns at the top of her lungs while doing the laundry and Raggs recites poetry whenever he has to climb a ladder. I'm afraid I haven't really seen any big changes, Mr. Masters."

"Well, I appreciate your help. If you think of anything else, just let me know. Good night. By the way, will Dotty still be awake at this hour?"

"She's a night owl – awake 'til the midnight movie ends. Her door is probably open. She hates having it closed."

"Thanks"

"Good night. See you at about seven in the morning."

She proceeded to the front door.

Masters was soon at Dorothy's open door. He knocked even though she saw him approaching.

"Come in."

"Hope I'm not intruding this late," Masters said, apologetically.

"I hate being alone. Have a seat. What brings you here?"

"The papers in your safe. I need to know exactly what they are."

"Let me get them. It will just take a minute."

She crossed the room, swung out a large picture and worked the combination. After a few moments she slapped the safe door and tried a second time. It opened. She was soon back with a shoebox full of papers and envelopes.

"I hate safes!" she announced, handing the box to Masters. "This is it. Much of it I may need to explain. Just let me know."

Masters donned some latex gloves and began going through each folded sheet and examining the contents of each envelope.

"One of those things, I guess," he said holding up two birth certificates.

"Yes, that would certainly be one of them. Alex has two birth certificates – one with the last name Lassiter and with Peter listed as his father. It was the original. Alex was born down in Joliet away from prying eyes so the name caused no interest. I checked into the hospital as Dorothy Lassiter. No one checked identities in those days. The second one has Adam listed as his father and uses the last name Williams. I made Adam promise before I agreed to marry him that the baby would have Peter listed as the father. I then agreed to Adam's demand that a second be drawn up with *his* name as the parent. It made sense since I had decided to let him grow up assuming that Adam was his father. He got a lawyer to fix things up. Whenever Alex needed a birth Certificate – like to enter school – we used the Williams document. It may sound more complicated than it was."

"I understand. I see you have several clippings from the old days. A prom picture with you and Peter I assume. I just saw his picture in Guy's room. Then there are these articles about Peter's trial. I must say it seems strange to keep something so morbid with your important papers."

"They contain the last pictures that were ever taken of Peter. I guess I have to plead sentimental value."

"I can understand that. You have some of Guy's papers in this one envelope – social security cards in both his old and new names, the name change document from the court, and his birth certificate."

"He needed a secure, fireproof place for them and rather

than have him go to the expense and bother of a safety deposit box at the bank, I offered my safe."

"That makes sense. I think that's all I needed. I'll leave you to your late, late, movie."

"Betty's been ratting on me," she smiled.

"You're right. And I plead guilty to listening. Good night."

Raggs crossed the entry hall as Masters descended the steps.

"Hot chocolate at ten thirty in the kitchen if you're still up at that time," he whispered as if delivering some great secret.

"What a wonderful way to end the day. I'll be there. In the meantime, where is the trash taken around here and when is it picked up?"

"There is a small dumpster beside the alley at the back of the lot. It is most easily accessed through the rear door of the laundry. Feeling the need to go slumming, are you?"

They chuckled together.

"What I'm feeling is the need to find the burned out light bulb from the attic – the one replaced recently."

"It will be my pleasure to escort you to the rear of the building. Trash pick up is early tomorrow morning so tonight will be the last chance."

"Well, we don't know when it was changed, of course. It may be long gone."

"But then again . . .," Raggs added.

"Yes. And that's what I'm counting on."

"Could you use a companion as you play in the rubbish, Sir?"

"Yes, but only if he calls me, Ray."

"I think he can do that now, Ray."

"In that case, break out the gloves."

Rubber gloves and flashlights were procured from a chest in the laundry and the two were soon outside. The back yard was lit brilliantly by two lights on poles sitting at opposite corners of the lot. The dumpster was near the alley beside a small garden house. A large white, two story wooden gazebo occupied the center of the area. Its generous use of delicate carvings and lattice work added a feminine touch not seen elsewhere on the property. It was surrounded by a sizable stone patio. A variety of metal chairs and glass topped round tables sat here and there as if awaiting a summer party.

Masters turned and visually inspected the rear of the house. He estimated it to be seventy five to eighty feet wide. Thinking about the inside he figured it must be close to one hundred and fifty feet long making the lot probably one hundred and ten by something over two hundred deep. The roof peaked at a low angle and a single, small, half-round window was set near the top of the sturdy rock wall, apparently more for architectural effect than to actually illuminate the attic.

Light shone from Alex's studio on the left side of the second floor. It was matched by lighted windows in Guy's room on the right. The two long, narrow, center windows – those from the study – were dark. Except for light coming through the small window in the laundry door, the lower story was dark.

"I'm confused, Raggs. Inside. The windows I saw on the east wall of the study?"

"They are shams, Ray – artificially lit from behind during the day to give the appearance of genuine portals to the real world. Actually they are set back into the not so secret, *secret room.* It is roughly ten feet wide and the length of the study - hall to back wall. Put in when the house was built as a safety haven from the senior Mr. Williams' ruffian business competitors, I'm told. It contains a narrow stairway with stops at Betty's office and then the basement. A door has since been cut into it from Alex's studio and he now uses it for storage."

"And the original entry points?"

"As if from out of a 1940's horror movie, there are sliding panels."

"No access to the attic?"

"No, I don't think so. One of my duties is to keep that

stairwell free from dust and cobwebs once each month. Another absurdity of my vocation since it hasn't been used in forty years. There is a set of pull down steps at the rear of Alex's studio but as Guy pointed out when we were in the attic, it only accesses the far eastern section. The wall between the secret room and the studio is stone and mortar from basement to roof. In the attic it becomes what Guy referred to as the fire wall."

"Helpful. Thank you for the tour and history. Old Mr. Williams Sr. must have run with the worst of them."

"That is certainly my impression, but little is ever said about him."

"To the dumpster, then."

Raggs threw open the lid. It was a small unit, perhaps two feet front to back, three feet deep and eight feet wide. Inside there were five compartments. Raggs explained.

"We are fervent recyclers around here – the one area Mrs. Williams and Alex insist on. The compartment on the right is for cardboard, to its left is paper, magazines and such, and then a section each for glass, plastic and garbage."

"Let's start with glass and see if we get lucky," Masters suggested.

They removed bottles, broken window glass, a punch bowl that appeared to have been punched once too often and, at the bottom, several light bulbs. It was Raggs lanky arms that procured them. As per Masters' suggestion he handled them by their metal bases.

"Bingo!" was Masters pronouncement as the third bulb was handed up to him. "An old Edison Bulb like the others in the attic. I assume there are none like those other places."

"Perhaps in the secret stairwell. I am not certain, but it will be easy to determine," Raggs answered, freeing himself from the dumpster.

"I wonder?" Masters said, standing back and surveying the dumpster. He began going through the section of papers. To his surprise, the third newspaper through which he paged contained holes - small sections had been cut out. Closer examination suggested they had been ads and he thought back to his initial conversation with Millie. Something about it had intrigued him since. He kept the paper. They closed the lid. It seemed to add credence to the idea Adam's murder was an inside job.

The men returned to the kitchen and placed the bulb on the table. Raggs rummaged through the cupboards.

"A few day-old doughnuts and a bag of pretzels are about all I find, Ray."

"If there's also that promised cup of hot chocolate, the doughnuts sound wonderful.

As Raggs brought the snacks to the table, Masters had to comment.

"Raggs, I declare. After twenty minutes in a dumpster you still look better than I do when I'm freshly dressed in the morning."

"It's simply a matter of orderly navigation through ones environment."

"Orderly navigation?"

The term itself produced a smile.

"Yes. Steering clear of hitches, snags and grime, and always safety-pinning your shirt tale to your underpants."

It was cause for a prolonged, tear generating, belly laugh for Masters. Raggs snickered but more at Masters' reaction than to his own, fully serious remark.

Face wiped and doughnuts dunked, Masters examined the old bulb. Burned out, alright. The filament is hanging loose. I loved these old bulbs as a boy. You could look right inside and see them doing their job. Today they're frosted or tinted or embossed or colored. Can't peek inside to make sure there's really a filament in there."

"But if they light, Ray . . .?"

"I know. I know. Faith in that which can't be seen. Always been a problem for me."

"You are a unique edition. There is no denying that, Detective Masters."

"I have decided to take that as a compliment and go to

bed. Well, perhaps just one more doughnut and then to bed."

The two toasted doughnuts and sat quietly, enjoying their growing, new friendship.

CHAPTER FIVE:
Day Two: Morning

Masters awoke hearing himself saying, "Date books are like prune Danish," no doubt the lingering vestige of some sleep-born idea about the hyphenated code. Before breakfast he entered the study and secured Adam's appointment book from the center drawer. He took it to the conference table in the rear of the room and sat, beginning to go through it day by day. The pages were numbered – something he had counted on.

"4-4. Let's look on page four for something else that is somehow four – the fourth line, the fourth letter, the fourth appointment, the fourth who knows what?"

He had hoped something would just jump off the page – perhaps underlined letters or words from which the first or last letters would somehow make sense. There were no such things. Masters was convinced the 4-4 sequence represented the letter I. The page contained many I's but none seemed to be attached to a four of anything.

If that weren't a hyphen but a minus sign 4-4 would equal zero and get him nowhere even faster than his present course.

Failure – *new challenges*, as Masters preferred to think of such things – always made him hungry, so he headed off to the kitchen, realizing he had failed to ask about breakfast the night before.

Betty was there, bright and early, as promised. She seemed to be satisfied with a cup of coffee. Perhaps she had eaten at home. Millie's greeting was animated as usual. Mr. M! So you're an early riser, too. Should a knowd."

"I just realized I hadn't asked about how breakfast is done around here."

"Any way you want it. Breakfast is pretty informal. Raggs and I eat at six thirty. Betty arrives about seven. Mrs. Williams – well she insists I start calling her Dotty so I will try – Dotty drops in about nine and Master Alex seldom arrives before ten. Mr. W. always had a tray in his study at seven thirty. Like I said, pretty informal. Whatcha like. I can fix anything."

"Pancakes?"

"Sure – buckwheat, buttermilk, blueberry or banana?"

"Blueberry-banana?"

"I should a figured. Bacon or sausage with that?"

"Yes," he teased.

"You're teasing the best teaser this place has ever known, Mr. Masters," Betty cautioned. "My advice is to watch your step. Once, when she was serving pudding, Raggs held out his cupped hands as a little joke. He got a hand full of chocolate pudding – two ladles as I recall."

Masters smiled enjoying that evidence of camaraderie amid the otherwise relatively sorrowful setting.

"By the way, the family priest is coming by at eight to make the funeral arrangements," Betty announced

"Priest? I wasn't aware they were Catholic."

"Big surprise to me, too, I'll tell you that," Betty said.

"Oh?"

"It's never been a religious, church going group around here – except for Millie. Not even Easter or Christmas Eve so I just assumed it wasn't a part of their life. I guess we'll find out when we speak with Father Guccionne - he says he pronounces it goo-chō-nee in case Italian isn't your second language. Dot had me call him yesterday. Apparently Adam's mother was a devout Catholic and Adam was christened by this guy. I assume that makes him ancient. Dot didn't know where else to turn."

"I'd like to speak with him after you have taken care of the arrangements."

"Okay. I'll tell him. My guess is he's probably a nice guy . . . that was a joke, folks – I don't attempt many so please pay attention."

It got the requisite smiles and chuckles and Betty seemed satisfied. She refilled her coffee mug and excused herself. Alone with Millie, Masters took time to explain the telephone code to her.

"Beyond this old head. Glad I could help get you going on it though. Raggs has the oven guy's promise to be here later this morning. I don't know what I'd do without Raggs. Don't know what I did before he came – of course I *was* a few years younger back then and Alex had a nanny "til he was twelve. That helped."

"Twelve. Seems a late age for a nanny."

"Mrs. Williams - Dotty – was so depressed during those years that she just kept her on out of desperation, I think. Alex had been kicked out of school that last year – seventy grade - so he had to be taught here. The nanny was a good teacher."

"Does that mean that by the time he was twelve, Dorothy had begun feeling better?"

"Not really."

She became all quite confidential.

"What it means is that one day she walked in on the Nanny and Alex while she was giving him his lessons in bed – if you get my drift."

"Yes, I believe I do get your drift. A lady's man from an early age, then?"

"Oh yes. Mr. W. acted like it was all a big joke – like he was finally proud of the boy for something. He even started calling him his little man. Dotty was so upset with all three of them that she took Alex to a hotel for a week. Of course she returned and nothing was ever said of it again. Alex had a male tutor for the rest of the term and then he returned to public school the next September."

"Changing the subject, Millie, something you said yesterday has been gnawing at my brain."

"What's that?"

"You said the words and letters used to write the threats had been cut out of newspaper *ads*. Not just out of newspapers. What leads you to believe they were from the ads?"

"The regular, stuffy part of a paper is printed in those little letters with the rounded edges – you know? But in the ads, the letters are often bigger and different styles. The ones on the cards was from the ads alright."

"Very perceptive."

He had wondered if initially the word '*ads*' had been a slip of the tongue, revealing that she knew more about the cards' origins than she let on. Either she thought fast on her feet and had just covered herself well or her explanation was the straightforward truth. Masters would reserve judgment.

Detective Killroy arrived.

"Morning folks. What a pretty day. I'm quite sure I spotted the sun for a moment there."

"Everybody's a comedian this morning," Millie said. "Eggs over easy, bacon crisp and toast, if I recall," She added.

"Yes. How nice of you to remember." Killroy took a seat.

"I see you've dined here before," Masters asked more to see what would follow than anything else.

"Millie was very kind to me at the time of the jewelry robbery."

Standing behind him, she rolled her eyes and moved to the grill.

"I have a few more pieces of info for us, Ray," he began, taking an envelope from his coat pocket. "No make yet on the prints on the new bulb from the attic. If they belong to a kid, we probably won't get an ID. The school records can't be used in criminal prosecutions of the children. Found two witnesses who say they saw Guy on the roof yesterday about mid-morning. The gardener at the house across the alley in back and the dog walker for the house to the East of here. Neither of them could be absolutely sure of the exact time but they independently placed him up there sometime between eight forty-five and nine fifteen."

"It's too big a time window. Keep looking if you will. What else?"

"I found a woman who knows a cousin of the carpet cleaners and thinks she can get me a phone number of the family in Italy. I need to call her later this morning."

"Good work. Anything else?"

"No. I guess that's it for now."

"We found a burned out light bulb in the trash that's identical to those ancient bulbs in the attic," Master said. "It's in my room and I'd appreciate a rush on printing it."

"No problem. You any closer to wrapping this one up?"

"Wish I could say I was. I decoded the first message – the one from the folder on his desk."

"You did! My, how I love this! *My* colleague on the case cracks the code while all the college boys down at the precinct with fancy computers and high powered software out their wazoos couldn't come close. This may be the greatest day of my life."

It seemed an overreaction but then Masters had never walked a day in Killroy's shoes.

"Would you be interested in what it said?" Masters asked trying to bring Killroy back into the real world.

"What it said. Oh, yes. What *did* it say?"

"G. Lester killed his nephew's father – APW"

"I see. Good work. No, I don't see. What does it mean?"

Millie inched a bit closer to listen as Masters explained.

"G. Lester is Guy. Adam is the nephew's father. Adam, you see was not Alex's real father. That was the older brother of Guy, making Alex, Guy's nephew. Adam accused

Guy of making the threats on his life."

Killroy clearly needed a score card. Millie couldn't contain her question. "Adam ain't Alex's father? Really?"

"Really. Dorothy confirms it. Let's not talk this about, however. She still believes that Alex does not know so we need to give her a chance to speak with him first."

"Oh, yes sir," Millie said. "Mum's the word."

Killroy nodded. "Yes. Mum, mum. Shall I arrest Guy?"

"We haven't a shred of solid evidence against him. You even found witnesses who say he was on the roof when the murder took place. What I need next from you and your men is a complete background check on Guy. Find out what you can about his recent activities, his friends and contacts away from here."

The men finished their breakfasts. Millie continued to look puzzled, sad even. Eventually Masters spoke.

"That second, hyphenated code is a doozie, I'll tell you that, Roy."

"That's a high class way of phrasing what the team of cryptographers in New York had to say about it. I won't repeat their exact words in the presence of a lady, Ma'am. I get the idea they have absolutely no idea how to attack it but they are willing to take our Midwestern money for a bit longer as they sit there on their patoots in their fancy offices staring at it."

"I worked out the first two lines. I'm sure it is the clue that will unlock the rest but so far I got nothing. It reads: *You see, dates like prunes, must be used properly.*"

"Well, too many prunes'll give you a good case of the trots – I can tell you that," Killroy said, perhaps or perhaps not trying to help.

"You may actually be onto something. *Properly,* in that context, may mean something like *in moderation.* How else could that be said? *Less than everything, less than all, less than the whole thing, partial or partially*? But see, it still seems to lead nowhere fast."

"Well, them prunes led somewhere fast, I'll tell you that

for sure."

Killroy was on a different wavelength and, apparently, felt completely comfortable there.

"Let's get you that light bulb," Masters suggested. "Millie, would you have a small box and some paper I could use to pack the bulb so it will be protected on the trip down to the station?"

She soon produced not only a six by six inch box but a small square of bubble wrap.

The bulb was procured and Killroy left. Masters decided it was time for another chat with Alex. He knocked on the closed door. There was no answer. Raggs was coming up the stairs and saw him standing there.

"Master Alex left early this morning with his lady of the evening – so to speak. Said he would be back about three. I can let you in if you like."

"I'm not sure I should enter without his permission."

"Mrs. W. – Dotty, and I will never feel comfortable calling her that – said that you are to have complete access in the house and that does include the studio."

"Very well. If you have time I'd feel more comfortable nosing around if you were with me."

"I'm taking quite a liking to this detective thing, myself. I think a butler is a natural. We are all given to snooping, you know. We feel offended if we are not the first to know things around the place."

While searching his pocket for his key ring with his left hand he turned the knob with his right and found the door was unlocked.

"I expected as much. Alex seldom locks the place. When the door's closed he wants his privacy. When it's open he's available. Is there anything in particular that we are snooping about for – My, my I do believe I ended that sentence with *two* prepositions. I'm becoming a bloody clone of Millie."

"I didn't promise that *good* things would rub off on you from your association with me," Masters joked. "In answer to your question, I'm not sure."

Masters began by just walking the room – round and round – back and forth – looking down and looking up. He stopped at the clay table and examined the huge clock.

"I don't know how this can be of any help to him. The knob that winds the alarm is already missing and I understand it's a new clock."

"Master Alex has always had a problem losing things," Raggs explained as if in defense of the man. "He was on a tear for three weeks trying to locate just the right kind. It had to be wind up since there are frequent power outages in this old part of the city. It had to have a huge face and alarm setting hand that set it precisely to the minute. I suggested a large faced digital clock with battery backup that I had found in a catalog, but once Alex gets his mind set he's a bugger – has been ever since I've known him."

Masters just listened.

"How do we get up to this attic?"

"The stairs are back in the corner. They swing down from the ceiling just as the others did," Raggs said walking to them. "I would not think he would lock them." He was correct, an easy tug on the rope, and down they came.

"No lock like in Guy's room?"

"Apparently, but not locked. First or second?"

"You go first. I'd hate to fall on you. Would not be a pleasant sight."

"Nor a pleasant experience, I imagine," Raggs added playfully.

They were soon upstairs. Raggs found the light switch. The attic was cluttered with small boxes and oil paintings – dozens and dozens of oil paintings. Unlike the far larger other side they had been in the day before, this side was floored. Again, Masters paced around. He examined the rock wall which separated the two sections of the attic. He examined the floor and the rafters. A hole in the floor caught his attention. It was the size of a quarter and surprisingly smooth around the edge.

"Mice, I imagine," Raggs said without being asked. "The exterminator does his darndest the third Thursday of every month but they are prolific little creatures."

Masters paced off its location from both the back and west walls. He shook his head as if to say never mind. They were soon back down in the studio. He looked up at the ceiling.

"Any trouble with roof leaks over here that you know of, Raggs?"

"None that I have heard of. Guy makes sure that part of the house is kept ship shape."

He looked through the things on the work tables, picking up this and that to examine, but finding nothing worth keeping. Mostly tools and carved, wooden, reverse images used, he assumed for making repetitive impressions in the clay – siding, bricks, stones, shingles, and several circular wheel-like pieces the purpose of which was not immediately apparent.

"Alex said if I wanted this reel of heavy duty fish line I could have it. I'm going to take him up on his offer. Let me leave him a note."

With that finished, the big man sighed.

"Well, I guess I'm done here. Like I said I had no idea what I figured I'd find and now, I have no idea if I found it."

"Am I to assume Alex is a prime suspect?" Raggs asked.

"No. If I were you, I'd assume nothing at all about this case. Other than knowing we have a crime, we have nothing but speculation, Raggs. Nothing."

As they walked to the door, Masters began thinking out loud.

"Mr. Williams had reason enough to think it was Guy who was after him to name him in the first coded message. But he left us no evidence to back that up. At first I thought perhaps the second coded sheet – the hyphen code – might contain that proof, but it was notarized four years ago. Unless he had believed for a long time that Guy had been plotting to kill him, that message probably does not hold the evidence we need. If he had suspicions for that long, surely some investigator would have been brought in sooner. Since Guy is the named suspect, I need to examine his room as well."

They walked to the opposite end of the hall and were knocking on Guy's door as Killroy topped the stairs and joined them. Guy opened the door, appearing happy to see them. With Killroy there, Masters thanked and dismissed Raggs.

"Come in. What can I do for you?"

"I need to look around in here, Guy. In a statement Mr. Williams left behind he named you as the person he believed was threatening his life. From your standpoint, the worst that my looking around can do is prove him right. The best may be to prove you innocent."

"Am I being charged with his murder?"

"No. No, Guy. There isn't a shred of evidence against you at this point. Anybody can accuse anybody of anything. It is only the proof that counts, and so far there is no proof against anyone."

"Well, I guess you either look now with my permission or later with a warrant. Go ahead. I'll just tell you ahead of time that the nudie magazines in the lower drawer wouldn't be here at all if Alex didn't bring a new one for me every Sunday evening. I'm not saying I'm not interested in women – I am – but I just wanted to explain that up front."

Masters figured if nudie magazines were the man's biggest concern, the search was probably going to end in another blind alley.

Masters perused the workshop table. Guy seemed to have every imaginable hand tool.

"No power tools?" Masters asked.

"I have a complete shop set up in the basement. Lots of power tools down there."

Masters continued to look around. A section of books – mostly on home repair topics – a few about lawn and garden care, one about chess for beginners. At one end stood a fishing pole and a small real of line."

"You a fisherman, I see?"

"When I get a chance. Fished the river as a kid. Still

enjoy it. I tried to get Alex interested but that's a no sale. Handling worms and slimy fish is not his idea of fun."

"How did you become so good at being a handyman?" Masters asked.

"Just by doing it. I was always the one who fixed things at home. Pete was all thumbs and Mom had trouble working the eggbeater. I just grew up loving this stuff. When Dotty married Adam, it was my ticket to be with her and Alex. I felt they were my responsibility with Pete gone. Dotty arranged things. I owe it to her. She is a wonderful lady."

"How do you feel about Peter and how things turned out for him?"

"How do you think? Mad as hell. Bitter as I can be. It eats at me every single day. If I could get my hands on the guys who really did those murders I'm sure I'd kill them on the spot and gladly take whatever followed."

There was a moment of silence.

"I guess that sort of flare-up doesn't exactly take me off the suspect list here, does it? I'm really a gentle kind of man – always have been. It's just this one thing, you know?"

"I can understand that if you believe your brother was set up, you'd be very angry about it," Masters said. "What about Adam. Did you have bad feelings about him?"

"Adam was always a jackass. I barely knew him as a kid. He had a short fuse and a reputation for getting back at folks he thought had done him wrong. I did know that much. He lived up here in the ritzy section but we went to the same school – his dad had something against private schools, I guess. So, ya, I never liked him and then when Dotty married him I guess I really started hating him . . . I'm not sure why."

"Oh, I have an idea you know why, Gus," Masters said.

"Okay, I loved her. I was so jealous of Pete when he was going with her I could taste it. Then after he was gone I got the guilts about how I had felt toward him – and her. I guess I still got them."

"Ever think about getting Adam out of the way so it could just be you and Dotty and Alex?"

"I'd be lying if I said I hadn't thought about it but that's a heck of a lot different than planning to do anything about it, you know."

"Does Dotty know how you felt about her?"

"You'll find out, I'm sure. It isn't *felt*, it's *feel*, and yes she knows. We've had a relationship for thirty years. It's the best kept secret in the mid-western United States."

"You're quite sure Adam did not know."

"He'd a had me killed if he'd a known. You had to know the man."

"I see. And Alex?"

"I love him like my very own, Mr. Masters. Our Sunday evenings together have been the highlight of my life all these years. Alex is as close to Pete as I can get, now."

"Alex doesn't suspect anything between you and his mother?"

"If he does, he has never so much as hinted at it. Since he keeps me supplied with his special magazines, I doubt it. I think he pities me because he thinks I'm a sex starved old man."

"And are you?"

"No, Sir."

"You realize that what you have been saying here provides a motive we have had not had before."

"Maybe, but think about it. I've really had a wonderful life here with Dotty. I love Alex. Would I throw all that away to kill Adam? And for what? The bad way he treated my loved ones? That only makes it more important that I make sure I'll be able to be here for them. Think what you want to, but I did *not* kill Adam Williams."

"How are you with puzzles and Cryptograms?" Killroy asked attempting to extract something of substance from the interrogation.

"Pretty good. Dot and I have spent many happy hours working on them over coffee in the kitchen late at night. What does that have to do with anything?"

"The death threats came as cryptograms," Masters

explained.

"If there are any ways to pull the noose tighter around my own neck, I seem to keep finding them, don't I? Do I need to get a lawyer?"

"It would be a good idea," Masters answered. "I won't ask any more questions of you until you do."

Guy nodded appreciatively.

"I'd still like to help you find the murderer, but all this seems to put a strain on that."

"Not necessarily," Masters replied. "Have you been thinking of ways that chandelier drop could have been triggered?"

"Well, yes but honestly, I ain't come up with anything. Actually, Raggs idea about having it tied to the cross beam with a bow knot makes the most sense except for the problem of getting up there."

"It appears that there have been ample opportunities for someone else to make copies of the key to the attic. With you on the roof, the person possessing such a copy could certainly have gained access," Masters explained.

"You're right about that, I guess. But it would need to be someone with some bulk. That couch is in the way of the stairs and it's very heavy. Some small framed dude just couldn't have moved it – not quickly or easily, anyway."

"Small framed dude?" Masters repeated.

"I keep thinking it's gotta be Raggs. It wasn't me. It wasn't Dotty. Alex wouldn't kill the man he believes is his dad. Millie is really doubtful – too loving, too small, liked Adam too much, just too not the killer type. Betty, well I figured she was his main lover. I know he had other women but I just always thought Betty was his main, go to girl, you know. I figured that would be too good a deal for her to bring to an end. That leaves Raggs."

"And he seems the killer type to you?"

"Well, no."

"And you know of some reason why he would want his employer of all these years dead?"

"No. It's just by elimination. He's the only one left. I like him – a lot. It's not like I want him to be the killer."

"Just your objective conclusion then."

"Right. My objective conclusion."

"I appreciate your candor and opinions about these matters," Masters said. He ushered Killroy toward the door. "Keep thinking about how the dropping of that fixture could have been triggered."

In the hall outside, Masters had another strange request of Killroy.

"Did you fingerprint the contents of the safe at the time of the robbery in Dorothy's room?"

"The contents were stolen. How could we have fingerprinted them?"

"The contents that remained behind, I mean."

"We printed the face of the safe and the handle, and every last piece inside – papers, mostly. There weren't any unexpected prints. In fact, hardly any other than Mrs. Williams."

"Hardly any?"

"There were a few underprints here and there – assumed to be people who had handled the envelopes and such before Mrs. Williams got them. Like I said the only other ones were underneath hers."

"Detective, I want you to have your print guy go over the contents of the safe again. Just the things that were in there at the time of the burglary. Can you arrange that?"

"Certainly, but what will I tell them? What reason should I give for having to do it all again?"

"You are the detective, Killroy. You don't need to explain why you want something done. You're in charge."

"Yes I am. I'm in charge. No need for explanations. I tell them to jump and they jump. I'll have him here within the hour."

Masters feared he might have just created a monster.

"And don't forget to keep searching for witnesses that might have seen Guy on the roof. We need the time pinpointed closer to 9:02 am."

"About that. I've been thinking," Killroy said as they made their way down the stairs. "He could have been sitting up there on the roof just waiting for the meeting to start and then pulled the wire from up there. It didn't have to hang down by the window to be usable. He could have had it up there with him."

"If there had been any way it could have been the triggering mechanism you just might have a point."

Killroy was not sure if it had been a complement or not, but he smiled.

At the base of the stairs Masters took a small plastic bag from his pocket and handed it to Killroy.

"Fishing line. I want the lab to go over this for me. I've included a note to let them know what I'm looking for. Like usual let me know the minute you have anything."

Masters walked him to the front door and then turned and was headed back toward his room when Betty spied him through the open door to her office.

"Detective Masters, could you come in for a moment. I'd like for you to meet Father Guccionne."

It was the first time Masters could remember seeing a disheveled looking priest. His clothes were dirty, his hair uncombed, his unshaven face sported a three day growth. His face glistened with oil suggesting it had not been washed in days. Masters shook hands, privately wishing for latex gloves.

Betty continued.

"Father, this is Detective Raymond Masters who Dotty spoke about earlier. He wanted to meet you and I suppose chat a while."

"That's right. Would you have a few more minutes you could spend here with me?"

The man nodded. Betty spoke once more.

"I need to run an errand. You two may stay in here to talk if you want."

She left and Masters began.

"You knew Adam's mother, I have learned.

"Yes. She was a parishioner for many years. Her family was Italian and they were from that area."

"And your parish is where?"

"It's in the old Italian section about twenty blocks Southeast of here. Back when Adam was born it was mostly first and second generation Italian immigrants - myself included. I was young and eager to make a good life for all my parishioners. It was a rough area where although men still did attend Mass their religion was often left at the church door. I had good attendance – people still felt that obligation back then."

"I believe that was the area where Peter Lassiter lived wasn't it?"

"Yes. You know about Peter and Dorothy, then."

"Yes, she filled me in."

"Peter and his family were among the very few Protestants in the area. He'd drop by we'd shoot baskets out back sometimes. A nice boy in a very bad situation. He was an outsider for many reasons – religion, his lily white skin, his good English and poor Italian. The other boys gave him a very hard time. Peter didn't even get along well with his brother – I forget his name. They fought the bloodiest battles between siblings I have ever seen."

"Over what kinds of things?" Masters asked.

"Anything! Money, the car they had bought together, girls, sports – if one called the other out you could automatically expect blood on the infield before it was over. But I think I have side tracked you from what you had on your mind. I'm sorry. Please go ahead."

Masters sensed the man was becoming agitated by the turn in the conversation. The Father sat in silence. Masters pressed on.

"Do you believe Peter committed the murders?"

Father Guccionne stood and began to pace. He bit at his knuckles. His face became flushed and tears streamed down his face leaving visible, irregular, trails on his grimy cheeks.

"See me! I am a wretched human being. I have carried this burden for so long. The witnesses to the murders that Peter was convicted of – two men and a woman – were from my church. Immediately after the murders they came forward with their accusations against Peter. They also immediately came to confession. In those days most of my flock came to confession.

What a priest is told in the confessional is the most private, most confidential responsibility he has. It cannot under any circumstances be revealed. I will therefore only say this – and God forgive me even for this – I know that I should not. I know for certain that Peter Lassiter was not the killer – he was not even with the boys who robbed the store. In fact, I do know who the murderer is but I am forbidden to say. I knew all of this at the time Peter was convicted but I was forbidden to say. He could have been executed and I could not have lifted a hand to prevent it.

"Since then, as you have surely surmised," he held out his soiled shirt tail, "I have been so distraught that I cannot even take care of myself. The Church gives me menial duties but I ceased feeling like a priest years ago. I go through the motions hoping each day will somehow be my last. I cannot tell you more, but perhaps knowing what I have said, you can find the killer and the false witnesses and set the record straight. Alex needs to know. Dorothy needs to know. I must go now. There is no forgiveness for what I have just done here."

He strode from the room shaking his head and mumbling to himself. Betty returned.

"Well, *he's* an experience, isn't he?"

"A very sad experience. *He* is going to do the funeral?" There was disbelief in Masters' question.

"He's going to see that it is done. Apparently he isn't into funerals for some reason."

"It's a long story. A long, very sad, story. Betty, my dear, how would like to become my first lieutenant for the next day or so?"

"Like a junior detective, with a *Cracker Jack* badge, you mean?" she said as if assigning some degree of triviality to the offer.

"Like a full-fledged, very important, junior detective," Masters said in all earnestness.

"You are serious. Sure. Of course. What can I do? How can I help?"

Her presence took an immediate, serious turn.

"At about the time of Alex's birth – a few months before – there was a trial of a young man named Peter Lassiter in the south Chicago area near Father Guccionne's church. I need to find out everything I can about Peter and the circumstances surrounding his arrest and conviction. I need to know who the main players were in the case from witness to political bosses. I need to find his defense attorney – at the time a young, wet behind the ears, public defender no doubt."

"This sounds like it could be the most important challenge I've had in the past twenty years. My degree was in journalism. I don't know if you knew that. When I graduated, I worked a couple of years on *The Southside Sentinel* – a now defunct neighborhood sheet not far from that area. It was mostly Italian as I remember. This is going to be great! You just got yourself a Junior Dick, Ray."

"Can we do this without telling Dorothy or Alex? I can't explain but that *is* crucial right now."

"Not a problem."

Masters left and continued on to his room.

It was time to outline all the possibilities and sift what was useful from the clutter and dead ends. He removed his sweater, kicked off his shoes and planted himself in the chair by the window. The yellow pad remained on the desk. It was a time for thinking not writing.

First there is John - gentle, myopic, efficient, spineless John - or so I am told. He was the first to point it out that *his* is the best motive so far - a huge insurance policy. Betty had an additional, interesting take on it. He can just sit back and let the money roll in now that he has been relieved of the work load. He can vacation. Move to the country. Travel the World. He's a good ten years younger than Adam so even without the policy, at $750,000 a year, the next twenty or twenty-five years would have certainly produced far more money than that one shot policy payoff. Betty touted him as some kind of financial genius so he would realize all of that. No, John would have to have had some reason other than the policy for wanting Adam dead. Conflict over a woman, perhaps? Men have killed for that reason since the species began. So far only the poorest of motives and not a shred of evidence related to John.

Alex. Guy put it well when he said he didn't think Alex could kill the man he believed to be his father. Besides, he seemed to enjoy tormenting him so, and that would stop once Adam was dead. Dotty says he has a temper like Adam, but this was not a temper driven crime. Again, was there a conflict over a woman? That certainly could be a possibility although one might think that in all of the greater metropolitan Chicago area there should be enough women even for the two of them – perhaps not. Alex didn't need the money - at least according to Alex. Perhaps that needs to be independently substantiated.

Guy is the odds on favorite in terms of opportunity. He says the motive is not there and yet, seeing Adam mistreating the two people he loves most in the world must be considered motive. He has the know-how to rig the necessary device - whatever that may be – and has access to parts and tools and all the time in the world to install it there above his own room.

Another possible interpretation of Adam's coded message came to mind during the discussion of it earlier in the day. What if by the term *father* Adam had really meant Peter, Alex's true father. It would implicate Guy in Peter's death. That meaning seemed incongruous to the matter of the death threats to Adam, however. Unless, Adam had run across some proof of Guy's murderous deed and Guy had found out that Adam knew so needed to silence him. But, then, why forewarn Adam with threats? The theory complicates the case exponentially.

Of all the characters in this story, Raggs intrigues me the most. He accepts and clearly likes himself as he is. He takes neither himself nor his work too seriously. He seems to find ways of enjoying whatever task is before him. He doesn't seem to need lots of people in his life and yet gets along well with all those who are. As a proud father and grandfather it seems unlikely he would risk his reputation and freedom by committing murder – unless there is some powerful as yet uncovered motive.

About that: A mention in the will? Perhaps. With his son apparently a very successful lawyer, Raggs' financial future is unlikely to be a concern. With his college background he would have the skills to devise and rig the necessary mechanism. He would certainly have been able to schedule the opportunity to install it. But his almost immediate entry into the study at the moment of the murder makes it unlikely he could have been in the attic to unleash the chandelier. Perhaps he did the work and Millie pulled the trigger. They could be a team. Masters had wondered if there were more between them than just being fellow workers, but had not found a tactful way of inquiring. If fellow conspirators, then why would Raggs have placed her at Guy's door just prior to the murder? *Her* story was different. One would suppose they would have agreed upon some air tight alibi well in advance. They are both bright people. When all is said and done, Raggs would seem to have no motive, though he is clearly fond of both Dot and Alex, his feelings would not appear to be intense enough to be the lone vengeful angel in all of this.

Now, Millie is another matter. She clearly loves them both, but then she apparently had a fondness for Adam as well. Dropping a chandelier on the man's head just doesn't seem to fit her style though I have no idea what her style of murder might be. Quick, quiet and painless, I imagine. Of course, *that's* exactly how it was done.

Dotty had as much or more motive I suppose as anyone - she'll inherit a huge amount of money and collect on the insurance policy. She'll be rid of the man who has tormented her and Alex for well over thirty years. Her son's financial future will be secured. Her marriage to Adam just might have been standing in the way of her marrying the man she really loves. Perhaps a collaboration between Dot and Guy.

Or, Guy kills Peter to win Dorothy's hand but she unexpectedly gives it to Adam instead who Guy later kills, again in a belated attempt to win Dotty's hand.

Oh my! *The Orient Express.* Perhaps it has been a conspiracy among all or most of the household members. Each one contributing their own dagger in some way. Raggs the creative mind behind the device, guy the builder, Betty scheduling Adam away so the chandelier and desk could be rigged, Dorothy manipulating the meeting and who was invited, Millie the trigger puller and Alex, the one who relocated the desk. An interesting, though improbable, possibility.

Each member of the household seemed to have developed his own method of interacting with Adam. It was not a group relationship - just a series of individual relationships each severely limited in scope and function. Efficient, I suppose. As if Adam were the hub of a wheel and each of the others an independent spoke feeding into him. Now, just how any of that relates to his murder - if it does - is not clear. It does suggest that if they were all in on it, it may well have been for a variety of reasons - each one having his or her own. But that is getting me nowhere.

Betty is remembered in the will, apparently in a more substantial way then if she continued to receive her salary and "consultation fee". At least that is how she made it appear. Aside from gaining financially and reducing her day to day irritation from having to work with the man, her motives seem weak, but then money and irritation are not necessarily insignificant. She and Dotty are close. It could be a twosome except for the mechanical expertise they appear to lack.

Betty, Dorothy, and Alex?

Betty seemed to know more about the Peter Lassiter case than she let on. She immediately knew the part of town and its ethnic and religious make up of some thirty odd years ago. That was well before her reporter days. But again, a good reporter often must appear to know more than she knows in order to lull the informant into revealing information. Perhaps it was merely a practiced response. I wonder why she quite journalism and just how she landed here?

There are, of course, an unknown number of outsiders who could be suspects. I don't believe an outsider could have executed this without the help of a member of the household, however. Logistics were just too difficult. John and Betty had the most direct contact with the outsiders and business associates. John seems to have little access to things within the house. Betty, of course, does.

Alex seems to function in his own little world all quite separate from the household. He runs his own business and has his own circle of friends - women friends at least - I don' recall hearing about male companions other than Sunday evening Guy.

Alex's motivation might change dramatically if he, indeed, knew about his parentage. To put up with an unpleasant blood father is one thing. To put up with one who is a despised substitute is quite another.

The most bothersome part of this is that, Adam, a savvy, astute person, was so sure the threats had come from Guy as to be willing to name him in front the household, the police and me and commit it to writing if only in code.

Now here's an interesting twist. Perhaps Guy *is* the one who made the threats but *not* the one who actually killed Adam. Perhaps there were simultaneous murder plots afoot in this foreboding old house.

Raymond, sometimes you simply amaze me! If there is a way to make a case more complicated you always seem to find it or - facts being scanty - manufacture them!

Too many folks with good motives. Too many folks with access to the murder scene in the attic. Too many good suspects all alibied right there under my nose at the moment of the murder. None of those will be the routes to solving this one.

one. It will be the device itself. That, of course, is made more difficult by the fact that whatever it was has more than likely been dismantled by now and its identifiable parts scattered to the winds.

The simplest device - a rope threaded through the holes in the collar and chandelier pipe, secured to the two-by-four beam overhead in the attic and tied in a bow knot - is very likely not going to be the method of murder - though goodness sake its simplicity is tempting. That approach required someone in the attic to pull the knot. Unless that was Guy - which seems unlikely considering the eye witnesses - it did not happen that way.

Now here's an interesting idea. Guy and Millie. Guy set it up, had the couch moved out of the way and left the stairway down. Millie unlocked his door, climbed the stairs, pulled the knot loose, sequestered the rope among the pile of linens she was carrying, descended the steps, and hurried into the study, appearing to be there almost instantly. Afterwards, Guy then put his room back in order and the rope was disposed of.

Millie's motivation is relatively weak unless she knows something the rest of us don't - and that is quite possible. Something like Adam considering a divorce or disinheriting Dotty and or Alex or, for that matter the household staff in general. He had already dismissed John. No, the solution will lie in the triggering device.

"My old brain needs a rest. It must be time for the morning coffee break."

He wished he had not removed his shoes. They are the most difficult part of dressing for a portly sort. Had he not known where the kitchen was, that morning, he could have just followed his nose.

"What is that wonderful aroma, Millie?"

"*Swedish, Walnut, Rollups.* My mama's own recipe. Shortbread, walnuts, a sprinkling of coconut with a thick pineapple glaze inside and out."

Masters sat down and Millie brought him a mug of coffee and a handful of paper napkins.

"They are strictly finger eatin' delicacies – sticky as a mama bee at feedin' time - and I'm not about to make more laundry."

As if on cue and quite probably led by his nose, Killroy arrived with another envelope. He took a seat and seemed more interested in what he had to share than in the treats (well, at the outset at least!).

"It is the strangest thing, Ray. Those papers and envelopes in Mrs. Williams safe - they are filled with new prints. Prints right over Mrs. Williams' prints. They weren't there at the time of the burglary, I can vouch for that."

Not that Killroy's *vouch* really meant anything, but it was as Masters had expected.

"Have the prints been identified yet?"

"No. The officer is on her way downtown with them now. If they are available we should have a match soon."

Dorothy arrived. Killroy took a handful of treats.

"I'm about to get that Italian phone number I think. Gotta run. Busy, busy."

He was gone.

Masters told Dorothy what Killroy had just reported.

"To your knowledge has anyone at all had access to those papers since the robbery?"

"No, I wouldn't know who. I began locking the crazy thing from then on. Dumb, really, the jewelry was gone - like locking the barn door after the horse has been taken. No one else has the combination. It hasn't been opened since, except that one time for you. Nothing in there now that I use. Have you identified the prints?"

"There hasn't been time yet. Later in the day we should know something."

"You suspect someone, of course, or you would not have had it all reexamined," she said as Millie refilled the coffees and pulled up a chair.

"Yes, I'm quite sure, now, that I know who it was but am not ready to reveal it at this point. Proof is always better than even the best conjecture."

"How you coming on the hyphen-code?" Millie asked.

"It sets my head swirling to just have you ask the question," he answered, playfully.

"That bad, huh?"

"That bad, yes! Let me ask you two this: Do the words *dates* or *prunes* or the combination of the two bring to mind any connections for you with Adam? I'm not even entirely sure what I'm asking. I just can't milk any relevant meaning out of that hint that he provided. Did he use the phrase, *'You see,'* often or to make any certain kind of point?"

His questions were met with silence. Then Dorothy had a thought.

"When Alex was younger, Adam would say things like, *'You see, dummy,'* after Alex had made a mistake or error because he had not followed Adam's suggestion."

Masters winced. Millie looked down into her coffee and swallowed hard.

"Well thanks. It may mean something. Just keep working on it," he asked. "You have the funeral arrangements firmed up, then, do you Dorothy?"

"Friday morning at eleven at the church where Adam was christened. I'm not sure if he'd have wanted a Christian burial or not. We never discussed such things. Betty says it's not mentioned in the will. He seemed to have lost his religion long ago, but then look whose talking. He had no friends for pall bearers so Father said he'd round some up. Pretty sad not to have anybody who really wants to come to your funeral and yet so many who are happy you're having one."

"I'm sure there is no good time for this question, Dorothy, but have you ever had any strong suspicions about who may have committed the murders for which Peter was convicted?"

"Sure. Tony and Jocco. I don't know their last names. They had bragged before that they had killed people for money. That was common knowledge. They were older than Peter - maybe five or so years older. I'm sure they would have never admitted to anybody that they had done those two, though. It got to be such a high profile case. They probably slithered off into a cave somewhere."

"Were they questioned?"

"I imagine but I really don't know. Once the eye witnesses came forward it was all over. Why are you asking about it now?"

"Idle curiosity, I suppose."

He could see that neither of the ladies bought his explanation but both were too polite to question it. Masters thanked Millie for the goodies and was on his way to find Guy.

He was soon located in the shed at the rear of the backyard preparing to rake the leaves.

"Got a moment?" Masters asked.

"Sure. And if you'll take one of these rakes and I got all day."

They exchanged a friendly smile.

"What do the names Tony and Jocco mean to you?"

"Tony Blanco and Jocco Larossa. How did you dig up that scum?"

"I suppose that answers my question."

Guy raised his eyebrows without further comment.

"What about the eye witnesses at Peter's trial. Remember their names?"

"Like it was yesterday. Johnny and Kate Larossa and Ben Jacks. Johnny was Jacco's cousin. He and Kate had just got married. Jacks was a wino and lived in the alley beside the liquor store that was robbed. He'd have accused his own mother for a pint of gin – or less."

"So you suspect they were paid for their testimony."

"What's a stronger term than *suspect*?"

"I see. By whom?"

"If I knew that I'd probably be behind bars now."

"No idea's even."

"Well, Tony and Jocco - if they are the ones who really committed the murders. I suppose his cousin, Johnny, would a did it just to protect him. Like I said, it wouldn't a taken much to get Ben's testimony. Why you interested in all that now?"

"You never know when there might be an old score to settle. I have to look at all the angles on his one. An outsider might think there was no better way to hurt Dorothy or Alex than to kill Adam."

"I'd a expected better from you than that. I won't pry but when you can tell me what you're really up to please let me know."

It was Masters' turn to raise his eyebrows. He had found another bright and perceptive household member.

"Thank you. What you've told me has been helpful. I'll have to forgo the pleasure of raking for the time being - perhaps later."

He walked back toward the house, suddenly aware of the leaves on the ground. Shuffling through them reminded of him of boyhood leaf-forts, hedge apple wars and the late fall scent of burning leaves which often led to baked apples and mulled cider. For a brief moment his youth returned and he considered clicking his heals in the air. As the image of his adult silhouette returned, that urge passed, though with some somber reluctance.

CHAPTER SIX
Day Two: Afternoon

Lunch was uneventful. Well, that is not entirely true. Everyone, including Guy, was there at twelve o'clock ready to eat. It seemed no one wanted to risk missing out on the latest buzz about the murder. Even Alex showed up four hours before he had been expected, but then with Alex time was typically irrelevant.

As he looked around the room, Masters had to wonder, 'If not any of these, then who?'

An interesting possibility came to mind - humorous in a macabre sort of way. What if the new fingerprints in Dorothy's safe belonged to Adam suggesting that he had found out from the documents there that Guy was Alex's uncle? Perhaps it had also been Adam who rifled through Guy's cigar box. Fearing Guy's intentions toward him, Adam then conceived a plan to frame Guy for making death threats, arranged for the chandelier to fall by whatever means and with whomever's help, planted the incriminating wire and stick devise in the attic to implicate Guy and have him put away for attempted murder. He would have made sure the chandelier would miss him when it fell, and it would have, of course, had the desk not have been moved forward. Adam had been away, and his entry into the study at the time of the meeting was his first opportunity to be in there since returning. With the room rearranged for the gathering, and the details of the plot on his mind, he didn't notice the desk's position. There would have been no reason to check it. The chandelier was dropped, by whatever means, and . . . well, the rest is as it happened.

There were several problems - not with the plan, Masters rather liked it, in fact, but with its execution [so to speak!]. An accomplice would have been necessary to trigger the device and then to remove the triggering mechanism from the attic. Back to the same of set of problems: What was the device? Where is it? Who removed it and how? (Adam and Millie, perhaps? Intriguing!)

Masters suddenly realized the others were staring at him. Apparently he had been chuckling out loud.

Lunch over, Masters headed back toward his room. Killroy intercepted him by the staircase.

"Got the number in Italy. Had an Italian officer make the call. Found the carpet guys."

Killroy was clearly proud of himself and apparently satisfied with the completeness of his report.

"And what did you find out about the desk placement?"

"The desk placement. Yes. Well, the head cleaner guy said they had first put it back exactly where it had been - he seems to pride himself on getting furniture back exactly where it belongs. He even takes measurements and draws out a floor plan. I hadn't thought about that before. It must be a difficult part of a carpet cleaner's job."

He was off on another side trip through la la land.

"You said *at first*. It was then moved again I assume."

"Yes. Some guy came in just before they left and had them move it forward a considerable distance - something about a new, much larger chair coming."

"I see. Just 'some guy'?"

"I'm afraid so."

"Well, that would account for the three, rather than the expected two, sets of mover's prints. Anything else?"

"It was a beautiful wedding. Over a hundred guests from

seven countries."

"You married?" Masters asked, hoping to bring Killroy back to the States."

"No. I was never asked."

Masters had learned not to automatically be openly amused at the man's apparent attempts at humor. His restraint was warranted. Sadly, that one had clearly been serious."

"I found another witness," he added.

"Placing Guy on the roof?"

"Yup. Says he saw him here at exactly 9:02. He knows because he was playing walkie-talkies with his friend and he was to get his next message at exactly 9:03. He was hiding behind the shed by the alley looking at his watch and waiting. Apparently the bad guys were closing in so he had to remain very quiet, yet alert to everything that was happening in the area."

"You are speaking about a child, I assume."

"About ten, I'd say. Gary Price. Says he knows Guy - comes over and helps him with yard work sometimes - shovels snow in the winter. Earns a little extra spending money."

"How did you locate him?'

"Funny. When I got out of my car, he was sitting on the front steps. He asked me if I was a policeman. Kids like policemen. I said yes and I sat down beside him and we started talking. One thing just led to another. I said I was looking for witnesses who had seen somebody up on the back roof yesterday morning. He said if it was Guy that I was asking about he had seen him. Then he told me about playing walkie-talkies."

Masters sensed it was far too convenient. A spontaneous, after the fact, iron clad alibi provided by a kid who earned spending money by helping his good friend Guy.

"Have his phone number and address?"

"Yes, Sir, Ray. Right here on the back of my card."

Masters took the card and thanked Killroy for his good work. For that, he would bite his tongue later!

"Any word on the new prints from Dorothy's safe?"

"No. Some kind of little snafu, I'm told."

"*Little snafu*? I wasn't aware that snafus came in but one super size."

"It seems the prints were misplaced but the officer is backtracking and they should be found any time now. Something about switching cars when she had a flat."

Masters wanted to ask, 'Does that officer happen to be your sister,' but he didn't and felt proud of himself for his restraint.

Betty came in the front door.

"I may have something," She said, directing her comment to Masters as she approached. "I found an old contact at the Courts Center and she got me a transcript of the trial. There were several musty copies available - fifth carbon copies I assume but still readable. It's very short, I might add. The whole trial fewer than a hundred pages. I've seen opening statements that were longer than that."

"I took time to look through some of Peter's testimony. He insisted he had been playing cards with two friends that night. The friends were never found - never interviewed. They seemed to have skipped the country. I figured that by now they might have come back so I looked them up in the phone book. Would you believe I found them both - Carter Finkelstein and Bart Constantine. I have already spoken with Finkelstein and he confirmed he was with Peter playing cards at the time of the robbery. Apparently he and Bart were offered work on a strike stranded freight train. Being out of work, they jumped at the chance. Once in New York they signed on to work a ship to London. They didn't know anything about Peter's situation until after it was all over. They worked ships to South Africa and Australia and didn't make port back here 'til more than a year later.

"When they got back and went to their union office to look for work they were contacted by an attorney, offered three thousand dollars each to move to California with a promise of work when they got their. The next day they left again. Constantine moved back here about ten years ago and

Finkelstein a few years later."

"And they never tried to contact the authorities about Peter?"

"They were young punks, as Finkelstein described himself. They would never have initiated contact with the authorities - especially after poor Peter was beyond helping."

"Who is this Peter?" Killroy asked.

"Long story," Masters replied. "I'll fill you in later."

He turned back to Betty.

"We need to find Johnny and Kate Larossa."

"The eye witnesses?"

"Yes. They would be about Dorothy's age now, I imagine."

Raggs walked by, watering can in hand.

"Excuse me but were you asking about Johnny Larossa?"

"Yes I was," Masters said, surprised at his question.

"Well I don' know if it is the Johnny Larossa you are looking for, but that's the name of Millie's mailman friend. Is that about whom you are inquiring? He lives not six blocks from here - the return address on his recent birthday card to Millie. It's the butler thing, you understand."

"Well, it is unlikely, but who knows," Masters said.

"You and your butler thing wouldn't just happen to know the name of his deceased wife, would you?"

"Let's see, I believe it was Kathleen or Katherine. I can't be sure but Millie will certainly know. Shall I inquire of her?"

"No, like in horseshoes, close just may be good enough."

Masters and Betty looked at each other and said it in unison, "Kate!".

Killroy was confused. Not like his usual state of blissful confusion but clearly uncomfortable confusion.

"I must have missed something. You think that this Peter and the mailman's wife murdered Mr. Williams?"

There was an uncontrollable group snort and three individual attempts to muffle it.

"Again, it is a long story, Detective and I will fill you in.

It's a different case, actually."

He turned back to the others.

"Raggs, this seems to be becoming a game of long shots. Here's another for your butler thing. Any chance Dorothy's door lock was changed after the burglary?"

"Yes, sir. That very day, before noon in fact. Guy put on a new one. She felt so violated, I guess you could say, that we rushed in to do whatever we could."

"Was the old one fingerprinted by the police?"

The three turned and looked at Killroy. He smiled and remained silent, not recognizing that he been expected to provide the information. Raggs spoke again.

"I do doubt that. Burglaries are not responded to immediately in this area - there are so many and so few are ever solved. The first police contact was a patrol car that arrived well after noon, I'm sure."

"Would you suppose that Guy would still have the old lock or would that be long gone?"

"He's a packrat. It's probably sitting in a coffee can under his workbench in his room. There was nothing wrong with the way it worked, just that it had been picked."

"Raggs, would you be so kind as to accompany Detective Killroy and find Guy. Then see if that lock is still available and, if it is, Detective Killroy, will you please see that it gets fingerprinted without getting lost. We would be looking for a print that does not match any from the folks here in this household."

Killroy seemed to understand. Raggs would keep him on track.

"Just be careful not to touch it in the process of fishing it out," Masters cautioned as the two men began climbing the stairs. He wanted to make certain there would be no excuse for either accidental or purposeful handling of the gadget. The chances of finding anything useful were slim to none but then so far, things seemed to be going his was on the second case. Now if only some of that good fortune would rub off onto the first.

"What's the best way to trace Postman Larossa back to his original address?" Masters asked, thinking aloud. "Phone books I imagine," he said, answering himself.

"I'm on it," came Betty's quick response. Know a gal at the phone company. Let's see what she can do for us before I have to attack the phone book stack at the library. I'm sure their address will be here in the transcript. I'll just track them forward to their current address or backwards whichever seems to work."

"I believe you're really a reporter at heart, Betty."

"You could have fooled me, but it sure sounds that way doesn't it? Do you think there's a connection with Adam's murder?"

"In a *'round-robin-hood's-barn'* sort of way."

Betty looked blank.

"An expression we have back East meaning an unnecessarily complicated, convoluted path, perhaps even being only tangential to the original purpose."

"Good words. Where'd you go to school, Harvard?"

"Well, yes, actually, but I don't advertise it. Seems to distance lots of folks."

"University of Chicago, here. Same sort of thing. Seems like a lifetime ago."

"Tell me about it, *child*."

"Well, let me give Marge a call at Ma Bell or whatever it is these days. Oh, there is one other thing that seems a bit odd. When I was picking up the transcript the gal in Records said I was the second woman in two months who had come in for copies of that trial. Who else would be interested do you think?"

“I agree. Odd indeed. You didn’t get a name?”

“Of course I got a name. It’s public record. It was a Karol Sue Caruthers – about five four, short black hair, blue eyes, nice figure, in her late twenties, hardly dressed like a professional person. Said she was a writer working on a story about the case.”

“And . . . ?”

"No female Caruthers in the metro area with the first name of Karol or Sue."

"You think quick on your feet, Betty. Not one of Adam's ladies, is it?"

"None *I've* heard of."

"Alex?"

"Who can keep track!"

"Well, I have no idea what that may be about but thanks for the leg up. I'll certainly keep it mind."

Betty went into her office. Masters had skimped on lunch so headed for Millie's kitchen.

"Knew you'd be here early on," She said, greeting him. "You didn't eat enough to keep a kitten alive this noon. Figured you had things on your mind – the way you was chuckling and all. Real food or junk? Got soup left and in three minutes a apple pie."

"How about I occupy myself with some soup until the pie is cool enough to be sliced?'

"How did I know that?"

Millie giggled and ladled out a big bowl of the soup of the day. Masters made conversation.

"Johnny stop in this morning?" he asked.

"No. Left the mail in the box. Guess I must have offended him or something. He's really cooled it the past month."

"The last month, huh? Well, I suppose there are other fish in the sea."

"That must be where they are 'cause they sure don't come around here."

"Oh, I'm not so sure of that. I seem to occasionally bump into a distinguished looking gentleman in these very halls who I understand is single."

"Raggs. He's soufflé and I'm omelet, Mr. M. Way outta my league - though he'd be a great catch for the right gal. I'm grateful to have him as a friend but that's all it could ever be."

Masters had opened the gate. Now he would just sit back and say no more about it.

"I understand the funeral will be Friday morning."

Millie nodded.

"Did you ever know you should do something but really didn't want to?" She asked in response.

"Oh my yes - many, many times."

"This is one a them times. I'll go, on account of Dorothy and Alex, but I'd sure rather be getting root canal."

Masters thought it an odd response from someone who professed to have liked the man but decided to let it fall where it would.

"Surely Alex will go won't he?"

"I wouldn't try to predict that one. If his mom asks him to he will. I don't know if she'd do that. It'll be the all time smallest congregation at a funeral. Better call Guinness."

"Speaking of calls, did the oven guy come by?"

"Ya. He arrived right when he told Raggs he would. That Raggs has a way with people, you know. Took all of three minutes and the bill is seventy five dollars. I think I'm in the wrong business. At seventy five dollars for three minutes I figure I should be earning seven hundred and fifty bucks for this here pie."

Masters squirmed a bit, realizing that *his* usual fee would make even that seem like a mere pittance.

The conversation remained light. Turned out Millie had three sisters - all of them maids and all of them maiden. Millie was the youngest. Her father had been an engineer who ran off with his secretary soon after she was born. All she had left to remember him by was a photograph and a few of his old books. So, she grew up in a family poor of money but rich in love - to her the only really important thing anyway.

As Masters finished his pie and oooed and ahhed appropriately to Millie, Raggs and Killroy entered the kitchen with a small box.

"I do hope there is good news in that box," Masters said, expectantly.

"The lock," Killroy announced.

"Better yet," Raggs added, "Guy says he always wears

gloves when he works on locks because he's allergic to the graphite that he sprinkles in the mechanisms to keep them functioning smoothly. If there are prints they'll be here - smudged maybe but they'll be here."

Raggs had clearly begun taking his detective work quite seriously.

"Millie, don't you think these two deserve a slice of the World's best apple pie?"

"Sure do, and today it's only about two hundred bucks a slice," she replied.

The men looked at each other.

"Just kidding," Millie explained. "A little joke between me and the big guy here."

"We do need that print report ASAP, Detective Killroy," Masters said, urging him on toward some level of efficiency.

"Right after the pie. Oh, by he way. I got a cell phone call from the lab. The prints on the attic bulb belong to a gal of questionable rep named Lilly Baxter. Beats all. She lives clear up on the north side. Can't figure what business she might have had in this attic."

Again there was a chorus of muffled grunts.

"Perhaps she works for the exterminator," Raggs joked.

"I see," came Killroy's all quite serious response and studied nod.

"It's just too easy," Raggs said, looking skyward.

Masters smiled with the rest and turned back to Millie. "Lilly Baxter ring a bell?"

"Not really. Jack's had a parade of women through here since puberty. I wouldn't doubt if there was a Lilly or two among 'em"

"Raggs?" Masters asked.

"I only keep the name of the lady of the day in mind. It would get too cluttered otherwise."

"And today's?" Masters asked

"I must admit I do not believe she was introduced to me."

"Perhaps the most direct route is through the horse's

mouth," Masters said. "I'll go speak with Alex."

He left. As he walked to the elevator he wondered if perhaps there had suddenly become too many cooks in the kitchen on this case.

Alex was working on his spa sculpture. At the knock, he motioned Masters in.

"You work in latex gloves?"

"Ya. I like to work with my fingers rather than tools when ever possible. Fingers leave pesky prints you have go back and smooth over, so on big projects I break out the gloves."

"I've struggled with that problem myself but never thought of donning gloves."

"You came here for a lesson in sculpting?"

It could have been interpreted as sarcastic, had Masters been prone to hearing things that way.

"No actually, I came to inquire about one of your female companions."

"Okay, Ray!! Tell me what you need and I'm sure I can get you a perfect match. Blond, brunet. . ."

"You misunderstand. Not for me. I have a need to know if one of the women's names might be Lilly."

Alex kept working.

"I think her waist's too fat. What do you think?"

"Depends if you're going for the anorexic look or not."

Alex smiled.

"Okay. We'll leave it as is. About Lilly, may I ask why you need the information?"

"I would rather not say so as to not make any false accusations this early in the case."

"The case! A suspect of some kind? Can't be my Lilly. She cries when a plant loses a leaf. Lilly. A suspect. Not a chance."

"There is a Lilly then?"

"Ya. Lilly Baxter. I've known her about two - maybe three months I suppose. Came on to me in a bar. Last time she was here was last Thursday – we had a sleep-over, you might say."

"This may seem like a very strange question, but for any reason would she have been in the attic over the study?"

He stopped working and looked Masters in the face for the first time.

"In the attic? Of course not. I have no way of getting up there from here. In the attic? Yes, that is a very strange question."

"Let me ask one more and I'll get out your hair. Has she been left alone here while you were elsewhere or been out of your sight for a period of time?"

"She's an early riser. Always awake in the morning way before I am. I suppose she might have roamed the halls a bit if that's what you're getting at. I guess. I don't really know. It's possible."

"Thanks for your help. I'll leave you to your work. By the way, I really like how you've draped the hair across her forehead - the statue's not Lilly's."

Alex chose to ignore Masters' attempt at humor.

"Ya. I like it, too. When the water flows down her face from the spray above, I think that hair treatment will provide an interesting flow pattern."

"I didn't' remember there was to be water."

"Ya. From three curved pipes. She'll be standing on a rock in a pool. The pipes will fan out behind her."

"I wish I could see the finished product. Perhaps a picture."

"I'll try to remember."

Masters left. The questions had clearly bothered Alex. Why, was not clear. Could Lilly have been an accomplice of his? Could she have been working with some outside person and befriended Alex only in order to gain entrance for them into the house? Was she a mutual friend of Alex and Adam with some score to settle with one or both of them? Her prints place her there or at least prove she handled the bulb at some point in its travels. She will need to be interviewed. Masters returned to the first floor by way of the stairs, easily convincing himself that it represented his morning exercise.

Raggs had left the kitchen and Killroy was just pressing the last morsels of crust onto his fingers and into his mouth.

"Glad I caught you before you left," Masters said. "We need to talk with Lilly Baxter. We also need a full background check on her - especially known associates during the past . . . say, six months. I need it like yesterday."

"I'm on it. By the way, I got the idea you weren't sold on the kids eye witness account so I talked with him again. I checked out the store where he bought the walkie-talkies. Get this. He bought them no more than an hour before he spoke to me. Something fishy, it seems."

"That is exceptional police work, Detective. [And this time he would *not* need to bite his tongue!] I guess I need to speak with Guy."

"He said he would be working out back," Killroy offered, as he stood making ready to leave.

Masters left through the laundry and found Guy raking leaves.

"Got a problem I think you will be able to solve for me, Guy."

"What's that?" He kept raking, head down.

"Well, we have this boy - Gary Price - who offered an alibi for you at the moment of the murder but there is a problem with it."

"Oh. A problem?"

"Yes. The walkie-talkies he said he had been using at the time he saw you up on the roof, were not purchased until about six hours after the murder. I have to wonder why the boy would lie for you."

"I suppose you really don't have to wonder, do you? Okay, I bribed him to alibi for me. It wasn't like a lie in the sense I wasn't really up on the roof because I swear on my mother's grave I was. It just seemed like you needed the time to be more specific then the other witnesses could give you so I tried to help it along a little. I guess that's probably interfering with a police matter, isn't it?"

"Technically, I suppose. We won't mention it at this point. Let's wait to see how things wash out."

"I thank you for that. I'll speak with Gary and set him straight about it all. I shouldn't have involved him that way. He thought it was all part of a practical joke I was playing on my policeman friend. He didn't know what he was really doing."

"The sooner you can do that the better, I'd say."

"Yes, right away. He's home schooled so that won't be a problem."

"One last question, guy, does the name Lilly mean anything to you?"

"Sounds like a dance hall girl in a *Gunsmoke* rerun. No. Don't believe I've ever known a real life Lilly."

Masters acknowledged his answer with a nod and returned inside. As he began pouring a fresh mug of coffee there was a knock on the kitchen door. Millie wiped her hands on her apron and answered it.

"Delivery for Adam Williams. One large box."

"Bring it in. You can put it over there by the window. Anything due on it?"

"Nope. Says RCA - revolving charge account."

It turned out to be a heavy, two man box from *Burns Office Furnishings* in Evanston, up on the North Shore of Lake Michigan. Millie signed for it and the delivery men left.

"It seems to be a new desk chair, from the picture," Masters said. "May I see the paper work?"

Millie handed it to him and he sat down at the table.

"Five pages of computer printouts to get one box here. Oh for the simpler days of one hand written original and a carbon."

He thumbed through the sheets.

"This is interesting. It appears to have been ordered by phone by Adam two hours *after* his death. Call Raggs if you would and let's get this thing out of the box."

The call was placed. Raggs arrived. It was clear he had done such things before. It contained a very large, very comfortable looking, high backed executive-type chair with dark brown leather upholstery that appeared to be a good match for the chairs in the study.

Its arrival gave credence to the carpet cleaner's reason for having moved the desk forward. How anyone – except Betty, perhaps - would have known that it *had* been ordered was one problem. How it *could* have been ordered was another. Perhaps the date was wrong on the paper work.

Masters was both amused and intrigued. After the fact alibis and after the fact order placements. What delayed piece of evidence would turn up next?

"Shall I move it up to the study?" Raggs asked.

"If it's alright with you, Millie, I'd rather it remained right here for the time being."

"Can I sit in it?"

"I see no reason not to make full use of it," Masters answered.

"Then consider it has a home."

She sunk into its deep cushioned seat and twirled a bit this way and that.

"I could get used to this. It'd make a dandy apple pealin' chair."

"At this point it wouldn't surprise me to find that the Will has suddenly been revised and the chair has been left to you."

Millie wasn't sure what he meant but let it pass. Raggs had a better idea about what he meant.

"Things not falling into place, are they?" He asked.

"I just think I'm getting a handle on it and then I'm ambushed by walkie-talkies, leather chairs and a dancing girl. What a bunch of amateurs - these Graystone suspects. I'm used to better, I'll tell you that, but, still, they do seem to be leading me on a merry chase."

It was cause for a brief, self-directed, chuckle.

It was then that he noticed - for whatever reason - a small discolored spot on the outside wall beside the table. It was about the size of a nickel.

"Millie. This spot. Do you know how it got here?"

"Sure do. The old crank telephone used to be there on that wall. It hung from a single bolt drilled clean through the plaster and into a wood plug in the stone wall behind it. When the phone was removed, Guy filled the hole with patching plaster. It's never looked right, somehow. Even with who knows how many coats of paint it's had, it still bleeds through from the back. Guy says that's because the new plaster is made different, somehow, from the old, original plaster. "

Some days are better than others. This one was suddenly proving to be pretty good after all, Masters thought. He went back to see Alex. He was gone. Masters found Raggs and a flashlight and they entered the studio together.

"I need to go back up into Alex's attic. You need not accompany me."

He was soon poking around near the stone fire wall. Presently Raggs heard a joyful, "Hot digity," from upstairs. Then Master's face appeared in the stair opening. See a hammer or a small saw or a chisel down there. I think they may be underneath the table to the right of the clay table."

"Yes, Sir. Your choice. They are all here."

"Then let's have one of each. I need to make this rat hole larger."

"*Mouse* hole," Raggs corrected as he ascended the stairs. "We are afflicted with *mice* not *rats*."

Remaining waist high on the steps he placed the tools on the attic floor beside the opening and a few feet away from the MOUSE hole. He watched with some amusement as Masters sawed, banged and chiseled it into a six inch wide opening. Using a flashlight he then searched its interior.

"This is a double Hot Digity afternoon, Raggs and believe me every case needs one."

He removed a length of something from the space between the attic floor and the ceiling below and put it in a bag.

"Not sure what you've found but I can tell you one thing," Raggs said as they descended the stairs. "That new hole should scare the beejeebies out of the exterminator next month."

Masters chuckled.

"It's been my experience that few people really want to possess those beejeebies anyway, so perhaps I will have performed a laudable service."

Raggs smiled.

Masters asked, "When was the exterminator here last, by the way?"

"That would have been about five days ago – the third Thursday of every month."

"And he sprays or whatever in both the west and east sections of the attic?"

"That's correct as well as every nook and cranny of the cellar."

"So the device – whatever it was – would have had to be put in place after that time to make sure it was not found or disturbed."

"That would also seem to be correct."

"When did Adam leave on his business trip?"

"On Thursday evening – a late flight to New York City. Left the house at about ten o'clock."

The stairs were swung up into place.

"Now there is just one more item I need and I'll bet dollars to doughnuts it's here. I'm not entirely sure who may have left it here, but I'll bet it's here. I'm looking for the gear mechanism from a motorized toy - a toy truck maybe."

"Like this, perhaps?" Raggs said, removing an item from beneath the table from which he had commandeered the tools.

Masters took it into his hands and examined it. He went to the clay table and found a small round spool, perhaps three quarters of an inch in diameter - one which Alex apparently used to make impressions in clay.

"Raggs, please note that I am removing the toy gear assembly, this wooden wheel-like object, and this fifteen inch length of curved, half-inch pipe I found in the hole in the attic."

"Duly noted, Ray. This makes me a witness of sorts, is that the idea?"

"That is the idea."

"If you wanted a pipe-carrying toy truck with a spare wheel, I'm sure there would have been easier ways to procure one. My goodness, now I'm sounding like detective Killroy. Solve this case in a hurry or it will surely be the death of me as I've known myself all these years."

"Suddenly, I am quite sure that I do have the case solved, Raggs. In fact not only Adam's death, but the jewel robbery, who framed Peter, and who had him killed. With a little luck I'll produce that actual killer himself."

"And none of that is for publication, yet, I assume."

"You assume correctly. At this juncture it is much like a woman who will tell you she is all dressed except for putting on her clothes. I have the cases all solved except for a few pieces of proof."

"I see. Detective work is apparently nothing like I expected it to be. I guess I'll stick with what I do well."

"It appears there are lots of things you do well, Raggs – a Renaissance man, it seems."

"A dilettante may better describe me – I do many things, but I only intend to do one of them really well."

"I envision your quarters as being unique in many ways," Masters said.

"I occupy the suite just south of you. You must drop in later."

They descended the stairs. [Two *'exercise'* sessions in one day! That nearly makes it a *three,* Hot Digity, occasion!]

"I need that big chair carton for a demonstration later on. Would you help me tote it to my quarters?"

"After butlering, toting is one of my best things, Raymond. Ah ha! *Raymond.* Now that feels comfortable. *Sir* has been too formal, I will admit but *Ray* was just too informal. Now, *Raymond* - that is a perfect fit."

"So glad to have that settled. I wasn't aware how much it was weighing on your mind."

They exchanged simple smiles between friends. Masters did hope Raggs was not a co-conspirator in all of this. He had grown to genuinely like the man. He could envision the two of them on a fishing trip in the Ozark Mountains - both with poles sporting unabated hooks so their conversation and enjoyment of the natural beauty would not be interrupted by some pesky, passing, rainbow trout.

Betty called to Masters from her office door. Raggs continued to the kitchen to procure the box. Masters approached Betty.

"Lucked out again, Mr. M. Millie's Johnny appears to be the same Johnny Larossa who testified against Peter. His wife died a number of years ago but she *was* the second of the three witnesses. The Jacks man went to an early grave in a bottle - in the *obits* two weeks after the trial. Found dead in the alley beside the liquor store - alcoholic poisoning according to the coroner's report. One interesting twist. I spoke with the officer who found the body. As he recalls there were five empty bottles beside the body. They had contained very expensive vodka, if one were to believe their labels. It wasn't even sold in that area of the city. It was put in the report but apparently never pursued."

"Very interesting. You suspect that either he had come into some money and made the purchase himself or . . ."

". . . or, more likely I think, they were gifts to him from someone who wanted him to drink himself to death."

"So," Masters said, "We are left with one of the three witnesses and he just happens to have showed up here in time for all the fireworks. Do you think you could find out anything about his employment and transfer record with the Post Office - I guess that's *Postal Service* these days isn't it?"

"It should be public record. I'll make some calls. I'll tell you this, Mr. M, I haven't felt this vital in years."

"Go get 'em, Betty!"

"Yes, Sir!"

She shot him a playful salute which he returned.

Killroy re-entered the house.

"Back so soon?" Masters said, wondering just what he could conjure up to occupy the man for the rest of the day.

"Happy to report the lost is found," Killroy said without

elaboration.

"The prints from the papers in Dorothy's safe?"

"Yup. Right where the Officer thought they'd be - under the front seat of the patrol car with the flat. It had been towed to one of the city garages to be worked on. The car sort of got lost in the shuffle. The report shouldn't be long now."

"I think I may be able to save the lab guys some time on that lock. If they do find a good foreign print, I believe it will belong to Johnny Larossa. His prints are surely on file - he's a Postal Carrier."

"I'll call that in, right away. So it was this Johnny fella who did in Mr. Williams, huh?"

"Only marginally likely, but I do believe he stole the jewels. I suppose you worked the jewelry fences in this area of the city at the time of the burglary?"

"Sure did. Came up empty."

"Go in and talk with Betty. She's in the process of finding out where Johnny's previous delivery route was. Once you get it, work the fences and pawn shops in *that* area. You still have the insurance photos of the merchandise, I assume."

"In the file. Put them there myself. I'm on it."

He headed for the front door. Why didn't his words fill Masters with confidence?

"You may want to wait until Betty gives you Larossa's old route. And, I believe you were going to call the lab about Larossa's prints."

"Oh, yes. Guess I'm just still excited to be working a case with the famous Raymond Masterman."

The big man had to chuckle and he no longer felt the need to disguise it. Killroy smiled and moved off toward Betty's office. 'Masterman' went to the kitchen passing Raggs and the box on the way.

"May I help?" He asked.

"Empty, it seems to be a one man job. Anywhere special in your room that you want it?"

"Where ever you find room. For my demonstration, I am also going to need a length of string - say about twelve feet and something about six inches long that I can use to represent the Chandelier. Something else for the desk in the study"

"A small plastic soda bottle for the fixture and a cardboard box cut to the proper proportion would seem to fit the bill. I assume the inside of the box will become the stage-like setting for all this."

"Yes. Your help will be appreciated."

"Will you require the rafters in the attic above the room? Guy has some lath that would work well."

"Actually that will be helpful. We can make it a cutaway-like diorama of sorts."

"I'll see to it . . . Raymond."

Killroy appeared as Raggs left. He accompanied Masters to the kitchen.

"Got the route. Made the call to the lab. Got a call from the officers who went to pick up Lilly for questioning. She is gone. Her closets are bare. The landlady has no information. A small van arrived about an hour ago according to one of the neighbors and a man helped her load a number of suitcases. There seemed to be some disagreement between the two of them during the process. They put out an all points to the airports, Amtrak, and bus stations."

"I imagine she is long gone by now, but let's at least give it try. We've been fairly lucky today. Who knows? Did you get a description of the man?"

"Average everything, I'm afraid."

"And the van?"

"Illinois plates but no number. No markings on the vehicle, and the witness was an old lady who felt proud she knew to call it a van instead of a truck. She had no details to offer other than it was gray or blue or brown."

"Millie," Masters asked, sitting down at the table. "What does Alex drive?"

"That's like asking which shirt he's wearing. He rents a five car garage a block north of here. There is no Van, if that's your point."

"It was, and I suppose there are probably hundreds of

places in the greater metro area to rent one. We'll call that a dead end.

"You think it was Alex with Lilly, then," Killroy asked.

"I have no idea. He is the only household member who has not been here all afternoon. I'm grasping at straws."

"I do have one more thing on Lilly," Killroy said as if an afterthought. "She's a freelance investigative reporter. Sells her stuff to the national gossip sheets and sleaze papers."

"That adds an interesting twist to all this. Perhaps she is the one who received the other transcript of Peter's trial."

"Well, I'm off to the pawn shops," Killroy announced without acknowledging Masters comments, and left through the kitchen door.

"Coffee?" Millie asked, already well on her way across the room with mug and carafe."

"Thank you, yes. Millie, about Johnny. He's been on this route about how long?"

"Close to three months, I imagine."

"And he began showing some interest in things here in this house right away, did he."

"Well if you're considering me one of the things here in this house, then yes, I suppose so. What's up? He some kind of bad guy?"

She threw up her arms.

"That would just be me my luck!"

Millie was not one to beat around the bush.

"I have my suspicions," Masters said. "Did he ask about things other than *you* here in the house?"

"Well, I suppose a lot of things did come up while we talked."

"Things like Mrs. Williams Jewelry?"

"Oh! My God! Pardon me for that, Lord."

"May I take that as a yes?"

"I'm afraid so. I guess I've been *had*, haven't I? It's just not fair. He seemed like such a nice man and we did get on so well - while it lasted. I must say I had to wonder how a postman could just take a forty five minute break every morning."

"Did he ask about Adam?"

"Only in passing, I guess. Maybe at the beginning but then not really anymore. Has he did this to other places, too?"

"I don't know, but that's an interesting aspect for Killroy to look into. I'm sorry about how it turned out with him and in reality I don't yet have him nailed down as the culprit - but I'd bet my reputation on it."

"Then so would I. Kay Sarah, Kay Sarah," she said with a flick of her hand. Like you said, there's bound to be other fish somewhere. I just feel so stupid - that I helped him like that."

"Most of us have been taken in by a con man at some juncture in our life," Masters said trying to reassure her.

At that point Alex strolled in and helped himself to some coffee. He sniffed the air as if to ask what treat might be available.

"Got a piece of apple pie waitin' for you in the fridge." She turned to Masters in a confidential manner. "He's one a them that likes his fruit pie cold."

Alex pulled up a chair across from Masters.

"So how is the detective work going? About to close in on the bad guy?"

"Well, yes in fact. I imagine it will be all wrapped up by this time tomorrow."

"Really!" Alex did not hide his surprise.

"Any sneak previews for the family?"

"Afraid not. A few loose ends to tie up yet. Speaking of which, Lilly seems to have left town. Any idea where she may have gone?"

"Not really. She's the free spirit sort. Maybe I did hear her talking about a trip to LA. Maybe that was Megan. One tends to run into another, you know."

"Well, no, I must admit that has never been one of my problems."

"Except for Mother and Millie here, I've never found a woman worth her keep - all untrustworthy by nature and far too demanding. Of course I've never found a man I could trust either, outside of this house, I guess."

"I'm sorry those have been your experiences. You've certainly missed the best part of life I'd say."

Alex raised his eyebrows and Millie patted him on his shoulder. He looked up at her acknowledging her gentle touch and gently placed his hand on hers. The two of them clearly had a warm, loving relationship.

He had not commented on the recently arrived desk chair - something Masters thought strange.

"The desk chair that Adam ordered arrived today, but then I guess you noticed it," Masters began.

"Ya, I saw. Looks like a pretty good color match to the leather in his study. Too bad he won't be around to enjoy it. It's really big, isn't it?"

"Yes according to the manual that accompanied it, it gives massages, plays music, and has a telephone in one arm. I wouldn't be at all surprised if it'll do 45 on the open road."

Alex smiled at Masters' attempt at humor. No more conversation about it surfaced so Masters stood and excused himself.

"Until dinner, then."

CHAPTER SEVEN:
Day Three: Morning

By nine thirty his three buttermilk pancakes had begun to wear off so Masters found himself on the way to the kitchen. Betty had just come in the side door and Millie was pouring her coffee. Masters took a seat, looking around expectantly for some delicacy. It would be cinnamon rolls - thick, sticky, pretzel shaped cinnamon rolls.

Betty was overflowing with information.

"I've located Peter's cell mate - George Pauling. He's worked at a Salvation Army soup kitchen on the south side for the past fourteen years - apparently a reformed man. He has given me the name of the Chaplain who was at Joliet at the time of the murder. Rumor has it that he has some information about Peter's killing provided someone in authority makes the effort to ask. I imagine a police detective will have the best chance to receive it."

"Good going. Would you take Killroy down there ASAP. Joliet can't be but what, an hour drive from here?"

"Something like that. I'll be glad to. Where is Killroy?'

"He called earlier. He's on his way with lab reports. I expect him any minute. There will, of course, be a built-in cinnamon roll hold in his schedule, you understand."

"That'll give me a chance to take off my phone messages

and move some things from one pile to another so it'll look like I'm still working around here. John Haven called and said he was going to stop by later and get some of his papers and files. I'll have them on the table by my office door if I'm not here."

"I'll be on the lookout for him," Masters said. "I'd like to have one more chat with him anyway."

Betty left and Masters enjoyed his mid-morning snack. "You spoil me rotten, you know, Millie."

"Seems to me you need somebody to do just that."

"Glad you noticed." He patted her hand.

Killroy arrived and handed Masters several envelopes.

"You were right about the prints on the lock. One great big beautiful thumb print on the bottom edge - Johnny Larossa's. How did you know?"

"It's one of those 1 plus 1 things, Detective."

"Ah! Mathematical."

Millie served him a roll for which he nodded his thanks.

"I'd appreciate it if you'd accompany Betty down to the Prison at Joliet to meet with the Chaplain. Apparently he has some information about the Peter Lassiter Murder. I would suggest that you call ahead."

"Be happy to. Betty has the poop, does she?"

"Yes, everything we know. We just think the Chaplain will be more willing to talk with a law enforcement officer of your stature – A.S.S. and all."

"Yes, I can understand that."

"A second item. Have you sent officers to pick up Johnny Larossa?"

"Done. I assume he'll be down at the precinct by the time Betty and I return. Shall I bring him here?"

"That would make my life easier if it's possible."

"As far as our Captain is concerned, anything is possible for Raymond Mistress. I'll arrange to have a squad car bring him here as soon as he's booked."

Killroy continued enjoying his roll. Millie warmed his coffee. Masters excused himself and headed for his room. Raggs was just coming out as Masters arrived.

"I have taken the liberty to do some work on the diorama, Raymond."

"Come in and let's take a look," Masters suggested. "Hey! Great work, Raggs. More elaborate than I had in mind but the better the better as they say."

"I didn't know *they* said that," he teased. "The rafters are drying - I glued them together. They should be ready to set up by lunch time. I have them to scale, right down to the notch in the 2 X 4 cross beam.""

Masters continued to nod his approval.

"Now, I need several more little things," he added. "Something to indicate the stone firewall in the attic, up here on top - just the lower foot or so will do. Then I'll need a straight pin, a small needle, a drinking straw, and a round toothpick. And some needle nosed pliers. Also, two more little boxes to represent tables in other rooms"

"All procurable. It will take me no time at all."

"No hurry. By lunch will be fine."

Raggs nodded and left.

Now, Masters needed just one more connection and he'd have his cases all wrapped up. He hoped that either the Chaplain or Johnny would supply it. He dialed Betty's extension.

"Ray, here. Do you happen to know any names associated with the opposition business group back in Adam's father's day? I got the idea they were maybe gang related. Not sure if Adam Senior was a gangland figure or not."

"I know very little about all that. Dorothy would probably know better than I. I'll ask her, if you like."

"That would be helpful. As you have time. Seems I've placed a lot in your lap during the past twenty four hours. Thank you."

"Killroy and I are leaving now. The Chaplain seemed suddenly eager to speak with us when I mentioned Peter Lassiter."

"Let me know as soon as you know. In fact, a call would be good when you're leaving down there."

"Sure thing. Did I mention what a *hoot* this is? See you in about three hours - maybe less."

Masters needed to look over the latest lab reports and to consolidate his thoughts so, taking a lead from Dorothy, he found a spot in the most disagreeable corner of the sitting room.

Still no report on the prints from Dorothy's papers. The prints on the gun found in Adam's safe were of one Edward Patchel – a two-bit hoodlum in and out of prison all of his life. A new player and not entirely what Masters had expected. He would call the lab later with a few suggestions.

One interesting development on the lubricant sample taken from the East hole in the central pipe of the chandelier - it contained a huge amount of graphite. Masters considered the finding.

Someone clearly thought more lubricant was going to be needed than something like just plain 3 and 1 oil. That makes sense considering the extreme weight of the chandelier that would be pulling down on whatever had been slipped into that hole to support it. It would seem to make sense that the graphite would increase the slipperiness of the contact points. That further suggests that whatever or whomever pulled that pin - for lack of a better word - could not be counted on to have the strength or power to easily remove it. A young *woman of the week* or a willing neighbor boy, perhaps?

It fit well with Masters' conception of how the murder had been committed. The essential question came to mind. "What type of material would you need to lubricate?" Not wood or rope as it would be absorbed away from the surface. Metal! It all fit well.

He read on. The pipe that had been forced through the mortar in the back wall of the attic - the one with the wire running outside to the wooden handle beside guy's window - had many prints on it, many of them smudged but all belonging to the same person - Alex. Since it was identical to the brass pipe he was fashioning for use on the bronze statue he was creating, it would be expected that his prints would be on it –

assuming it came from – or been taken from – his studio, and that was the odds on favorite. One would suppose that he would have wiped it clean if *he* had placed it there. One would suppose that if placed there by some other perpetrator it would *not* have been wiped clean so as to implicate Alex.

It was essentially the same finding for the small curved length of brass pipe Masters had found hidden beneath the mouse-like hole in the attic above the studio. It was an ingenious place to hide incriminating evidence. Someone could have chosen that spot thinking it would be hidden forever there between the ceiling and floor. Who would think to go snooping in mouse holes for evidence? [Who, indeed!]

Masters dialed 67. A voice from behind him said, "You rang?"

It was Raggs who had entered the room in search of Masters and had arrived just in time to watch him dial.

"You really are very good at this butlering thing. I need your assistance with two more items. On the diorama I need to have the ceiling extended out in both the east and west directions to represent the areas over Guy's room and the studio.

Raggs was immediately on it.

"A large piece of cardboard can be cut to size and placed atop the main box. That is no problem. And the second thing?"

"Millie says you're the go to man when a metal detector is needed.

"Oh, yes. A pastime of some years. I've found some interesting things - old coins, cartridges from prohibition days, a belt buckle supposedly hand made for Al Capone. But, how can I put it to work for you?"

"I need you to go over the attic above the study. I'm looking for a small metal rod or pin not quite three quarters of an inch in diameter and with a hole of some kind in one end. When you locate it you'll need to handle it with gloved hands. I assume it will have been heavily lubricated so you can expect to have rock wool insulation stuck to it. Leave it attached. Then draw a floor plan of exactly where you found it and its orientation. I'll come along for moral support and such."

"*And such* meaning you'll be looking over my shoulder to see that I don't do anything nefarious?"

"I'd rather think of it as protecting your behind in case there is a question about your honesty."

"Than neither I nor my behind shall be offended." He winked at Masters. "You sound quite sure that we will find this little rod."

"I am quite sure it exists and I assume it remains in the attic. Whether or not we find it depends on your gadget and your skill."

"I assume there will be hundreds of nails in the ceiling lathe. It will be a challenge, but I feel up to a good challenge today. Shall we do that now?"

"It's good for me."

"Give me ten minutes and I'll meet you in the upper hall."

Raggs left and Masters dropped off the reports in his suite. Guy was just leaving his room as they approached, and helped by pulling down the stairs for them. He would be in the basement if needed.

The two men were soon in the attic. Masters believed he could speed up the process.

"May I suggest you begin in the area right over there," - he pointed.

Raggs donned a set of earphones, pressed a red button and then began adjusting a green knob as he made slow even sweeps back and forth in front of him. A few minutes later he stopped and put the unit on the floor. He got to his knees and began fishing through the insulation off to the south of the walkway.

"I believe you would call this either a *Bingo* or a *Hot Digity*, Raymond. It is right here."

He pulled a glove onto his right hand and reached into the insulation. He placed the little rod end to end between his thumb and index finger.

"About four inches long, a half inch or a bit larger in diameter. Looks to be a shiny metal of some kind. Heavily lubricated and coated in rock wool. You have a bag, I assume."

"Right here my friend. Let's take a look, first."

They moved under a light. Carefully, Masters brushed the insulation away from each end. One end was rounded and well lubricated. The other was cut flush as if from a larger rod. There was an eighth inch hole drilled through it about half an inch back from the blunt end.

"Looks to be stainless steel - not a common type of rod. Might be a door pin for a refrigerator. Can't be sure. Probably to wide for that unless it was a commercial unit like for a restaurant or hospital perhaps and look at the edge of the small hole, Raggs."

"I see. It's as if filed smooth for some reason – very smooth."

"At any rate, we now have the last physical piece of this puzzle," Masters said with a satisfied nod.

"Good for us?" Raggs said with mock enthusiasm, knowing full well he had heard all he was going to hear for the time being.

Raggs soon had the sketch completed and the two were back in the hall on the second floor.

Masters couldn't resist pulling Raggs' leg.

"Just to set the record straight it is a *Bingo* when a piece of evidence is located and a *Hot Digity* when some aspect of a case suddenly falls into place. Since the existence of the rod was already part of my solution, it could not qualify as a *true* Hot Digity but stands well as a full fledged Bingo."

"I do appreciate that clarification. I shall enter it in my journal and study it dutifully."

That fishing trip began looking better and better to Masters. Realizing there could be no useful prints on the newly discovered rod - the oily insulation having obliterated any that might have been there - Masters had no need to send it to the lab immediately. He returned to his room to work some more on Adam's coded letter. There had been no progress update from the specialists in New York City so he assumed there had been none.

Masters sat at the desk and began writing on his yellow pad - all the time muttering.

"I'm sure I know what it says and yet I can't prove it. There is only one kind of information that he would have disguised so well. I'll write down my version of its contents now, and hope there is some break before I have the rest of the case wrapped up."

Five minutes later he tore the sheet from the pad and locked it in his briefcase. He stared briefly at the coded message and threw up his hands. Our system of numbers functions in groups of tens and the metric system in units of one hundred, but this one appears to be based on thirteen - the first set of numbers in each hyphenated set is always some number from zero through twelve. A bakers dozen - perhaps it was devised in a kitchen. The second half is from zero to nine. That would be a ten base system. Perhaps it has to be read in reverse some way. It is mind boggling."

His phone rang. It was Millie.

"Mr. Haven is here and he found a note on top of the things Betty had set out for him saying you wanted to talk with him."

"Yes, thank you. I'll meet him in the sitting room. Give me five minutes."

Masters noted that John seemed less agitated than at their first meeting but then his former partner had just been murdered so perhaps that was reasonable. He stood to greet Masters as he approached. They shook hands and sat.

"Betty tells me you have been the financial genius behind the big profits for *Williams Furriers* all these years."

"I'm not sure about genius but I have had very good fortune in making investments. It's self-serving, of course. The more the business makes the more I make. How is the investigation coming?"

"Very well actually. I do need some information about Adam's - how shall I put this - about any less than legal connections he may have had."

"The Syndicate?"

"Whatever."

"Adam played the fringe between legal and illegal. He was not to my knowledge involved officially in any aspect of organized crime. Some of his associates were of the unsavory variety. His father before had been in deep. I think he advised Adam to steer clear of it all. If you are asking if the crime organization had something to do with his death, I cannot say. I know they shared some of the same women - that's more than enough as I understand it. I doubt if they would pussyfoot around with threats of any kind, let alone coded messages cut from newspapers. Sounds far too juvenile and unprofessional, I think. They would be more *bim, bam, boom* direct."

"The business is still sound financially?"

"Oh, yes, and becoming more so every quarter. I don't know how that could have played a part in all of this. I just canceled my life policy - the one with Adam as beneficiary – and I must say it gave me quite a sense of satisfaction. Our attorney says that the Will is going be read on Friday afternoon right after the funeral. It's probably good to get it all out of the way in one shot. Nobody liked Adam but just to get it all settled will be good. The contents of his Will hold no surprises for the family - Adam made no secret of his intentions. A few of his lady companions from years past may be offended however. I think he promised them big things and they will find they get nothing - well there is a trust arrangement of support but it is not associated with the will."

"Now that you've had time to reflect on things do you have a favorite candidate for the murderer?" Masters asked.

"It's such a toss up really. If ***I*** didn't do it then the two next best suspects would be Dorothy and Betty I suppose. They are both dear girls but they had so much to hate about Adam. Dorothy and the fact he kept the other women and the terrible way he treated her and Alex and how he dominated them. Betty for the same plus the substantial monetary windfall she is to receive at Adam's death."

"That large, is it?"

"I estimate both women will both end up with a fortune in the vicinity of thirty million dollars."

Masters raised his eyebrows.

"Betty? Did she know?"

"I assume so, though I can't be sure. She did all of Adam's confidential paper work. There is a sizeable lump sum upon his death and then a quarter of a million dollars each year thereafter. I believe she meant more to him than his poor wife ever did. It's ironic in a way. The two most important women in Adam's life have become best friends these past few years and *he* had neither one for a friend. There was something in his make-up that would not allow him to remain close - emotionally, I mean - to any woman –perhaps, to anybody. Maybe he felt vulnerable in that kind of a relationship and Adam would not allow himself to feel that way for long. He was very self-protective - like an island fortress. It was like there was some good in him but it was burred so deep it seldom surfaced."

"I hadn't realized you were such a student of the human psyche."

"Ten years in Analysis tends to you make one that way."

"Yes. I would imagine. What is your take on Dorothy and Betty as co-conspirators in Adam's death."

"No twosome had more reason to want him dead yet no twosome could be less likely to have seen it through. They hated him no doubt but their kinds of hate would be so intertwined with compassion that they could never have pulled the trigger."

"And then there is Alex. Any perspectives on him?"

"Behind his ready smile and charm lays a man every bit as despicable as his father. He is self-centered to the point of destroying anything that interferes with the fulfillment of his slightest need. He has everyone around here conned. His father used women and then cast them aside. Alex uses women and then beats them to a pulp; he has never held his liquor well."

"My. You present a side of Alex that I have neither suspected nor heard about."

"He holds the record for the number of out of court settlements for battery, Mr. Masters. Our business attorney had him as a client during his adolescent years but dropped him cold when he reached eighteen. And when a lawyer is skittish about a client you know how bad it must be."

"I had heard Alex sported a temper, but I just didn't suspect such an ongoing problem."

"He was such a disappointment to his father. I will say that Adam shielded Dorothy from the gruesome details of their son's darker sided. I suppose that's to his credit."

"Three more names on my list. Guy, the handyman; Millie; and Raggs."

"Guy is a loner. I have suspected that he and Dorothy had a romantic relationship but I have nothing to actually base that on. Just the glances I saw exchanged between them, the way their faces would light up when the other entered the room."

"Do you think either Adam or Alex suspected that same kind of thing?"

"I doubt it. They were both too self-absorbed to pay attention to such things. I don't know Guy well. He seems distant. I have seen him overreact sometimes to little things – like hitting his thumb with a hammer or misplacing a tool. It has been my experience that outbursts which are so out of proportion to the cause, most frequently come from folks with some deep seated anger or rage, which at other times they manage to control, through constant vigilance.

"Raggs is a gentleman from one end to the other. He seems to be living a self-imposed exile from women companions, although if he would just give his feelings free reign I believe he'd discover that he is extremely fond of Millie. They are miles apart in many ways but in terms of being just plain good people they are a fine match. Could they be in on any of this? I doubt it.

"Raggs is not given to expressing his feelings openly so

it is difficult to feel his pulse about things. He came here under strange circumstances as I recall. He sent a letter of inquiry about a position as butler when there had been no consideration to add such a position. Then, not waiting for a reply he showed up on the doorstep and requested a meeting with Adam - of course he asked for Mr. Williams. Adam refused to see him so Raggs just marched into his study, closed the door behind him and thirty minutes later, Adam was introducing him as the Graystone's new English Butler."

"Any ideas what changed Adam's thinking?"

"One of two things. Either Raggs convinced Adam that he appeared to others to be far less of a man - a successful man - than he should, since his home lacked the distinction of boasting a professional butler *or* he was able in some way to blackmail him. Ego and threat - the only two meaningful motivators for Adam. I'd not play to his ego and had nothing to threaten him with. You can see where that left me."

"With about ten mil in the bank - as of Friday afternoon - and close to another million in dividends every year for the rest of your life, the way it looks to me," Masters said, answering quite pointedly what John had certainly intended to be a rhetorical question.

"You suggest there is a third way to Adam's heart - becoming indispensable."

Masters nodded.

"Do you know why Adam sent for me," Masters asked and then clarified. "How he came to know about me?"

"Our lawyer's son-in-law was aware of your work back during your days on the force in New York City and I believe you and he have a mutual friend. When Adam asked for the best, you were recommended. Adam never traveled second class. If your retainer is insufficient, I can take care of that for you."

"The fee is fine - undoubtedly far too large according to *the price per slice of apple pie scale*."

John's brow furrowed.

"You had to be there, sort of," Masters explained, not

really explaining at all.

"One last question and you certainly don't have to answer it if you don't want to. If you had decided to kill Adam or to have him killed, how would you have gone about it?"

"What a delightful question. The first thing that pops into mind is that I would have somehow arranged to infect him with some excruciatingly painful, fatal disease, but one that would have allowed him to linger on in agony for years."

"Have you considered writing mysteries or horror stories?" Masters joked, his expansive abdomen jiggling as he chucked to himself.

"It does appear that I have some flair in that direction doesn't it? If that's all then, I'll be on my way."

"Nothing else. Do you know yet what you're going to do from here?"

The man smiled broadly.

"Some years ago I made a copy of Adam's little black book. I think I'll try mining that for a few years."

"You old roué, you," Masters said, taken by surprise.

"You know what they say about us quiet guys!"

He winked - an unexpected gesture - and left the room.

Masters had to wonder just how much of the conman had rubbed off on John down through the years. It had been a useful interview although Masters was not entirely sure how much of it he wanted to just accept without independent corroboration.

It was lunch time - in fact, almost past lunch time. Masters hastened toward the dining room. Again, it was just Millie and Raggs at the rear table. Masters acknowledged them with a wave and went to work filling a plate.

"We was about to send out the hounds to find you, Mr. M." Millie joked.

"Yes, my missing a meal would probably justify that. Looks wonderful. A south of the border buffet. What is this marvelous smelling soup?"

Raggs answered. "*Minestrone, Ole!*"

"*Southern* Italy, I assume. Hope I'm not interrupting anything intimate, here," Masters said intentionally stretching the nature of the relationship. He continued before either could respond.

"I've come across some information that suggests Alex has a darker side I haven't been told about."

The other two looked at each other. Millie sighed deeply. Again it was Raggs who spoke.

"He has had a history of violent behavior but when you said this was not a crime of temper, I guess we didn't feel the need to elaborate. He has gotton himself into jam after jam because of his violence. I understand he was asked to leave one of his elementary schools for beating up a teacher during class and there have been numerous instances I am aware of since coming here - mostly violence against his female acquaintances as I understand it."

"Has he ever struck out at you or his Mother, Millie?"

"Never, so far as I know - not against me for sure. It is so unlike the Alex I know that it's just hard to believe. It's so sad."

"I know all this is hard on you but bear with me if you will. Have you noticed any change in the behaviors of either Alex or Guy since the burglary?"

They looked at each other, thinking. Millie had something on her mind. It was clearly difficult for her.

"It seems to me Alex has seemed less agitated recently. Maybe that isn't the right word. It's like he's felt more peaceful or something. It's hard to describe. I figure he's finally started to act his age, maybe."

"How about Guy?"

"Guy is just Guy," Millie said. "Ask him to fix something and he gets right on it. None of his regular jobs are ever left undone. He never makes no demands. I guess he's been more skittish since you arrived. But then he's been a prime suspect. I guess that would make you gun shy wouldn't it?"

Raggs cleared his throat.

"I have noticed that he seems to be around where people

are more than usual. He comes to lunch - first one here today, in fact - things like that. It's hard to judge someone's feelings when they don't talk, but he has seemed happier to me the past several months - this last month in particular."

"Ya. I seen it too," Millie said, agreeing with a nod.

"A butler is expected to keep household matters confidential but under the circumstances I suppose this needs to be said, just to you, Raymond. About three weeks ago, I was on my way to dust the study early one morning - perhaps six o'clock, before Mr. Williams arrived for the day - and I saw Mrs. Williams coming out of Guy's room - in her night jacket."

"And you were surprised at that?" Millie asked.

"Perhaps not, but I had never before witnessed what I may have suspected."

"Do you two have an opinion as to whether or not it was the two of them who murdered Adam?"

Again they looked at each other across the table.

"I'd like to say a definite no," Raggs began, "But at this point things seem so confused that some days I have to wonder if it might not have been Millie and I who did the deed."

Millie smiled and reached across the table to pat his hand. He accepted it as if perhaps it weren't an unfamiliar gesture.

Raggs excused himself. Soon Millie followed suite and began clearing things up in the dining room. No sooner had Raggs left than he returned.

"There are two uniformed police officers here with Mr. Larossa, Raymond."

"Thank you. Show them to some corner spot in the sitting room. I'll be right there. Thank you."

"Thumb screw time for Johnny, huh?" Mildred said her sadness showing through her lighthearted reference.

"I prefer the cattle prod," Masters said, hoping to lighten the situation even further. Quite clearly it didn't and he excused himself.

"Masters approached the three men in the sitting room and took a seat."

"The Captain said you wanted to chat with Mr. Larossa, here," the older of the two policemen said as if needing to provide an explanation of their presence."

"Yes. Hello, Johnny. I'm Ray." He extended his hand and it was accepted with clear reluctance. "I am a private detective working for the folks here in the Graystone. We know you stole the jewels a few weeks back. We are close to finding where you sold them. I assume it was revenge against Adam Williams for one of several possible reasons - shabby treatment in the past for services you rendered him, I imagine. We have a print placing you at the scene and will soon, as I said, have a positive ID from your fence. How am I doing so far?"

Larossa remained silent. The second policeman said, "He gave up his right to counsel at the precinct."

"Let *me* continue then if *you're* not in the mood to talk. At this point we have jewel theft against you. Mr. Williams was murdered earlier this week. Would you like to try for murder one as well?"

"I didn't kill nobody. You was right. Years ago I did some things for Mr. Williams from time to time. There was one pretty big thing once and he never paid me for it. Said he'd implicate me if I ever said anything and he could have, so I let it go. When I stumbled onto him here on this route and the maid confirmed who it was, I figured a guy owning a place like this was worth a fortune. I sweet talked her into telling me things. One day I just walked in clean as a whistle and took the jewels. The lock on the door was a joke and the safe was open and everything just like Millie said it would be. Easiest heist in history, I thought - 'til these guys showed up on my route and cuffed me. But you can't pin no murder on me. No, Sir. I don't know nuttin' about no murder. Not that he didn't have it comin' but I didn't do it."

"And have you heard anything on the street that might be helpful in our investigation?"

"No. I swear. I don't run with that crowd no more. I got a good job with a pension coming and my nose has been clean for twenty five years."

"That's true according to his rap sheet," the older policeman verified.

"Let me make a suggestion," Masters said, addressing the three of them. "Why don't you go back to the precinct and get a statement down in black and white - both about this robbery and about every single thing Johnny ever did for Adam Williams. This is not just another run of the mill case, Johnny. The whole force is out on this one. Whatever you did for him we'll find out one way or the other. I'm sure your cooperation up-front will not go unnoticed."

Then he addressed the policemen.

"I will get a transcript the minute it's available, correct?"

"Yes, Sir. I'll hand deliver it day or night if that's what you want."

"Thank you. That *is* what I want."

"Oh, I almost forgot," the younger policeman said. "I have an envelope for you from the L. G's."

"L. G's?"

"Sorry. *Lab Guys.* It's a local thing I guess."

They put on their hats and the three of them left.

They had been gone less than ten minutes when Raggs arrived.

"Betty on line one for you. That means you press the button labeled one and say hello."

"That much I do remember, Raggs. . . . Hello, Masters here."

"We found Peter's killer. He died some years back but gave the Chaplain a full confession with a proviso."

"A proviso?"

"Yes. It was understood that it would not be revealed unless it was specifically requested by the authorities. The Chaplain was plainly relieved to get it out of his files and into Detective Killroy's hands. There are some interesting twists but I get the idea that you already have them figured. Be back by one thirty or so. Did John Haven come in?"

"Yes, he picked up what you had left for him and he and

and I had a nice long chat. He turned out to be a different sort than I had expected. Well, I'll see you in about forty five minutes. Who's driving, by the way?"

"We are being chauffeured by the Captain's own driver. I'm beginning to see that definite benefits accrue from working with Raymond Masters."

The old detective smiled and hung up. Raggs had remained in the room but at enough of a distance to provide Masters with his privacy.

"Anything else I can do to move things forward?" he asked.

"That piece of cardboard to extend the attic floors on the model."

"Done. I took the liberty of gluing it in place. Should be dry. I also set up the rafters. Looking good if I do say so myself."

"Thanks, Raggs. That should do it for now. I'll be in my room. Have Betty call me the minute they return."

Raggs nodded and left. The next several hours should have things wrapped up. Masters figured he deserved forty winks and was soon back in his room doing just that.

CHAPTER EIGHT
Day Three: Afternoon

The phone rang rousing Masters from a heartburn driven dream about adobe haciendas, castanets, and bronze skinned, Mexican, dancing, girls.

"Masters here."

"Betty. We're back - in my office. Here or there?"

"I'll come to you. Give me five."

Their information began with, *"Here's Pauling's confession about killing Peter,"* and it just kept getting better from there.

Betty was the spokesperson for the duo.

"He names the man who set it up, details how his wife received a new car and $5,000 in cash before the hit as payment."

"The name of the contact?"

"Jules Rafferty. The Chaplain said he was a well known hood who had, somehow, managed to stay out of prison. He was the only name on Pauling's visitor list other than his wife's. Pauling died eight years ago in prison - doing life for another murder."

"Does this Rafferty ring a bell, Killroy?"

"Not with me. I talked to my Captain and it did with him but no connection with any boss type or gang."

"Have them ask Larossa if it rings a bell with him."

"Right now, I suppose?" Killroy asked.

"The sooner the better, detective."

The call was placed. Killroy's face lit up as he strutted back to where Masters and Betty were sitting.

"Are you ready for this?"

Masters spoke, "You mean are we ready to hear that Larossa has already admitted to having delivered the pay off to Pauling's wife by way of Jules Rafferty and that he did so while in the employment of Adam Williams?"

Killroy did a double take.

"Why yes. That's what he's said, alright."

Betty nodded.

"Now I see where you've been headed, Ray. Adam had Peter killed in prison. I still must be missing something here."

"Peter was already convicted but was awaiting appeal. If, on the slim chance someone came forward that threw a monkey wrench into his conviction, there was a chance he might go free. If he did, Adam felt he had no chance of getting Dorothy - just about the only thing in his life he hadn't been able to get if and when he wanted it. With Peter killed, he felt sure that Dorothy would be his. He was correct. Larossa contacted Rafferty, who was not connected in any direct way to Adam. Rafferty delivered the payoffs to Pauling's wife. Pauling then killed Peter. Adam won Dorothy's hand. Later on, Pauling apparently got a case of the guilts and made the confession to the Chaplain with the proviso we've heard about. Pauling would not have known about the Adam connection."

"So, Adam in effect killed Peter," Betty said pulling it all together. "Do you think that is somehow connected to Adam's Murder?"

"Oh, yes, my dear. But there is more and I am counting on Johnny Larossa to provide it. Thanks for all the help, you two. Couldn't have got this far without you."

Many things zipped over Killroy's head but never a compliment.

"I sure do thank you for that, Mr. Maltese. Just doing

my duty as a duly authorized law enforcement officer."

"There is still the matter of Adam's murder," Betty asked more than stated.

"I have that well in hand, Betty. I'm just waiting for one more piece of testimony and I'll be ready to put it all together. In fact, why don't you go ahead and arrange a get-together for all of the principals for nine o'clock this evening in the study. Stress that means nine o'clock *sharp*! Millie, Raggs, Dorothy, Guy, Alex, Havens, Yourself, Detective Killroy and his Captain, and someone from the State's Attorney's office.

He turned to Kilroy.

"Detective, I will need certain rooms to be cordoned off as crime scene area – immediately - with uniforms stationed to see there are no trespassers. Let's see, I'd say four should be enough."

"Got yellow cordoning tape in my car."

Masters was surprised he hadn't produced it from his inside, jacket pocket. He made his request more specific:

"Guy's room, the study and the studio. If Guy and Alex need to get any necessities out of there places allow that, now – inventory what they take - but then absolutely no one in unless they are with me.

"Got it. On it. All but done. Did you say four uniforms?"

Masters nodded and turned to Betty.

"Where did Adam get his liquor?"

"*Martin's Liquors* on the Northwest side."

"Always?"

"Usually. Almost always. He runs a tab. I pay it every month. What's going through your head?"

"That's quite a ways from here. There are bound to be dozens of liquor stores between here and there."

"A family tradition I suppose you could say. Adam's father owned it. Adam sold it as soon as Senior died - along with a world of other assets not strictly associated with the business. That's second hand from Dorothy, you understand."

"How do you feel about tracking down the longest long

shot anybody's ever pursued?"

"I'm game, but again, I'm two steps behind you, I'm afraid."

"You have some sort of access to Adam's early check books, I imagine."

"John never allowed any scrap of financial paper to be discarded."

"See if you can determine if Adam or some household member might have purchased a quantity of vodka on or about the night of Mr. Jacks' death. You know the date and the brand and amount of vodka."

"You're going to nail Adam for Jacks' death as well, aren't you?"

"*We*, my dear. Old detective Raymond Masters and the recently re-born ace investigative reporter, Betty Lyons."

She smiled and administered an unexpected but immediately welcomed bear hug.

"Records that old have been put it on microfilm. Should be a snap to locate if it's there. Then verify the sale at *Martin's* if I can, right?"

"You think like a detective, my dear."

It was a toss up between finding a place to think, and ferreting out a snack [for mental energy only, of course!]. Masters decided both might be available in the kitchen. He was right. Millie seemed to be elsewhere and the note on the table indicated there was a frozen lemon dessert in the freezer for any who might require sustenance [well, the note actually read, "Lemon Squares in freezer if your guts growlin. Help yourself and clean up your mess."].

It was and he did.

Several things about his talk with John Havens had been gnawing at him. One was the phrase relating to the act of killing Adam - *'Pull the trigger'*. Clearly the man had not been shot. The usual generic term might have been *Pull the plug*. In fact, the gadget as Masters had recreated it did involve *pulling a trigger* in a way. It was nothing incriminating but still a bit disquieting.

The other thing was just more of general interest. The way he spoke of Alex and Adam's relationship certainly gave no hint that he had any idea they were not father and son. If John had played any part in the murder it would have been based on something other than that.

Raggs entered the kitchen carrying a box containing a dozen, small, round plastic kitchenware containers.

"Raymond. A little early to be snacking, isn't it?"

"Mental energy, Raggs. I'm in need of a quick surge inside this old head."

Raggs noticed Masters' unspoken interest in his containers. He sat the box down on the table and began removing the lids.

"Lint, Raymond. I must admit it, I'm a lint junkie."

He put the back of his wrist to his forehead mocking the melodrama heroin in her moment of crisis. Then he explained.

"I make lint pictures."

Masters frowned but cocked his head in interest.

"Rather than paint, I glue various colors of lint onto the canvas. Ever helpful Millie dries like colored clothes together and then gathers the lint for me. Once a week I come in to claim it. She leaves it for me here on top of the fridge. Let me show you."

He took down a large old aluminum cake pan and placed it on the table.

"I see," Masters said, understanding at last. "I've never heard of your art form."

"I'm not sure it's widely recognized as *art*. When my son was in preschool, his teacher used it as a project. I became intrigued by its possibilities and got hooked. My rooms are rampant with them."

Masters looked through the selection that Millie had saved.

"Every tone imaginable. Who'd have thought? From brightest white and yellow through the more somber tones."

A small clump of dark gray material in one corner caught Master's eye. He reached in and felt it between his fingers.

"Is this what I think it is?" he asked holding it up for Raggs to examine. He transferred it to Raggs palm.

"Certainly looks like rock wool insulation to me, if that's what you're getting at. That Millie doesn't miss a trick. It will be a wonderful hue for shadows on the side of a mountain peak."

"If you don't mind, I'd like to keep it for a while – just until I can ask her if she remembers where it came from. Notice how it appears different as though it has not gone through the wash and dry procedures. It is as if she may have hand picked it off some article of clothing before adding it to the load."

"Certainly. Keep it. My mountain is very patient. Should you want to view my artistic creations, I would be pleased for you accompany me back to my quarters."

"Yes. Thank you, I would like that. I need a few tidbits of information I thought you might be able to provide. We can kill two . . . I hate that saying but my brain insists on starting it whenever the situation comes up. My gray matter seems to be in an irreversible rut."

"I like to think of it as the over-efficiency of the mature brain. It supplies phrases out of habit so we don't have to spend time scouting about in there for them."

Masters shook his head and they were off in the direction of Raggs' quarters. He had not overstated it. There were pictures on every wall, sitting on every flat surface and available from a number of partially closed chest drawers. The clutter was fully incongruous with the Raggs known by the household. As Masters prowled the room, hands behind his back admiring the work, he talked.

"How did Betty come by her job here?"

"When the former secretary - Beatrice Higgins - retired, Adam had her find her own replacement. She had been with his father and then with him. After an exhaustive search and dozens of interviews, Betty was the one she selected. All pretty straight forward I believe."

"And has she proved worthy, would you say?"

"I really couldn't say. My duties are quite separate from the business. She is pleasant and efficient and to my knowledge Adam seldom raged at her. I suppose that is the ultimate commendation. A bit reserved but, then, I should talk, I suppose."

"And you, Raggs. There seems to be some mystery surrounding your being hired here."

"Oh, really. No one has ever asked me before. I suppose it could be considered a bit unorthodox – gruesome even to some I imagine."

Masters' interest clearly grew.

"A little less than forty years ago, Adam killed my father in a hit and run accident in London. I spent some time searching for him and eventually located him here. When my wife died and my personal situation called for a change, I decided to play my ace, so to speak. In England there is no statute of limitations on leaving the scene of a fatal accident. I sequestered a letter containing the necessary proof, came to the States, confronted Adam and agreed to his very generous offer to be his butler. It had been an accident. My father, in fact was intoxicated at the time so the death was far more his fault than Adam's. Still to protect his interests in London he decided he needed a Butler. I did not threaten to expose him – just let him know that upon my death the evidence of his connection to the death would be revealed with ironclad documentation."

"I didn't hear any of that, you understand," Masters said, opting to ignore any legal ramifications that might relate to such a set of circumstances. "You held no animosity toward Adam, then?"

"Some, I suppose. As a young man I had a few fantasies about making his life forever difficult, but that passed. By the time I arrived here, it was more a matter of personal, financial security than anything else – it is a life-time contract in good health or poor while he lives and after his death – a trust. I have never asked nor taken anything more than the local going rate for the type of services I provide. In fact, initially he offered more but I turned him down. He never understood that. The poor man."

"For the record, Raggs, did you kill Adam Williams?"

Raggs smiled through an extended pause.

"If I did I would say no. If I didn't I would say no. My answer, my friend, is no."

Masters would not pursue it. Raggs had clearly and tactfully demonstrated the absurdity of the question.

"You do magnificent work, Raggs. These paintings or whatever you call them are splendid."

"I guess I have never really considered what they should be called, but I suppose technically they are not paintings are they - perhaps *lintings* would be more suitable."

Masters frame shook at the humor of Raggs' interesting taxonomy.

"Are they for sale?"

"No. I give them as gifts. How can one sell a labor of love?"

Masters nodded, expressed his appreciation for the tour and information and took his leave. He headed for Betty's office.

"Just the guy I was looking for," she said. "This may be what we're after. Same date - a check for seven dollars and twenty eight cents. Would that have bought five fifths of quality vodka back then?"

"You're asking me as if I would know from first hand experience," Masters joked. "Yes, my dear, believe it or not it would have."

"I have to find the ledger Beatrice would have entered that transaction in. She was the secretary here before me. It will be in the vault in the basement. I hate to go down there. Spiders, mice – gives me the willies."

"Perhaps Raggs would make the trip with you. He's great moral support and I have the idea that he could vanquish the most vicious spider in the place."

"Okay! Okay! I'll do it myself. Be back in a few minutes."

"Before you leave, do you know the particulars of Raggs contract?"

"Yes. Interesting. It's a 'get-paid-'til-the-day-you-die' contract. Has a yearly raise schedule based on five percent above any increase in the national cost of living. He's also in the will for several hundred thousand dollars. One strange twist. Only Raggs can break the contract but in return for the lifetime contract Raggs agreed that he would not resign until after Adam's death. Like an indentured servant, of a kind."

"And Millie?"

"As far as I can tell she doesn't even have a contract. Just agreed to work here and has ever since. Adam gave her better than modest raises. He knew she was a valuable commodity."

"Know anything about Alex's finances?"

"Not really. He's a corporation. I know he takes in millions every year. Aside from his cars, women and law suits, he really seems to spend very little money. I suppose he's got quite a stash somewhere."

"I'm not sure how to ask this one. Has Alex ever made advances or less than descent proposals to you?"

Betty smiled and patted Masters' arm. "Honey, except for his mother and Millie, Alex hits on every female he comes in contact with. Sure he has. I've always stayed my distance. He's not a nice person. I don't need that in my life for any size payoff."

She shuddered – dramatically - and left for the cellar. It was not entirely clear if that reflected her feelings about Alex or the spider infested cellar – perhaps they produced the same reaction.

Masters had some preparations to make prior to the evening gathering. He returned to his room to work.

Within the hour his phone rang. It was Betty.

"You hit it on the head, Ray. That check number matches the purchase of five fifths of Leningrad Vodka. I made a few calls to liquor importers. They agreed that back then it was only sold in high class outlets on the northern fringe

- where the disenfranchised aristocratic Eastern Europeans had begun to settle."

Masters thought out loud.

"So Jacks drank himself to death on five fifths of a rather rare vodka not available in the Little Italy area. He would have had to travel across the entire length of the metro area to buy it and then exercise the necessary restraint to take it back to his home area before drinking it. Doesn't sound like any wino I've ever run across. Thanks again. You'll make photo copies of the relevant paper work for me?"

"Already done and waiting on my desk."

"I get the idea Beatrice Higgins was a very good judge of secretarial potential when she hired you," Masters said.

"Either that or she was my Aunt Bea – take your pick."

Again, Masters' body shook as he enjoyed the humor implicit in Betty's remark. He hung up and immediately called Raggs, requesting that another large box be brought to the study. He finished up the several small projects in his room and went upstairs. The uniformed policemen were in place. He shook his head. They each looked about fourteen. My how time plays strange games with ones perception.

Raggs arrived dragging a four foot high box behind him.

"Will this meet your needs, Raymond? It is the largest I could find. Guy breaks them down for recycling almost immediately. This one is the box in which he saves those he's taken apart. I left a bit of a mess in the basement, I'm afraid."

"Looks perfect. He can have it back tomorrow. Let's just place it here beside the desk for now. We will need chairs arranged again much as they were at the Monday morning meeting. There will need to be ten this time."

"I'll take care of it at once."

"If you can remain here for a short while. I will need your help with one more matter."

"Certainly."

Masters moved on to Guy's room, climbed the stairs and was soon in the attic beside the chandelier hole. He crawled form place to place, stringing the fish line he had procured thanks to Alex's generosity. At last he called down through the chandelier hole to Raggs.

"I'm going to drop a fish line down to you. Please make a small hole in the center of the solid top of the box – with a pencil, perhaps – and somehow secure the line in that hole."

A minute later Raggs had completed the request.

"All set here, Raymond. Anything else?"

"No. That will be all. Thanks."

Raggs arranged the chairs and left. Masters worked a bit longer and then moved on to the studio. Again he entered the attic and again he crawled here and there. An hour later, he closed the studio door behind him and returned down stairs satisfied he had everything in order for the rapidly approaching get together.

Killroy was standing patiently in the entry hall much like a faithful dog awaiting the return of his master. His face brightened when Masters arrived. [Again, much the face of . . . well, you understand.]

"I have the last of the lab reports and the full statement from Larossa."

He handed several envelopes to Masters.

"My boys keeping the crowds away up there are they?"

It had been a joke. Masters followed his lead and chuckled with him.

"Still nothing from the cryptographers in New York?" Masters asked, sure that he knew what the answer would be.

"Nothing. My Captain called them about an hour ago and they are completely baffled. Maybe it's not a coded message at all but just a joke of some kind."

"What an interesting idea, Detective," Masters said. "The ultimate put-on . . . or put-down. A way of saying, 'See, I am better than all the rest of you'."

Killroy felt he should be pleased but was not sure why. Before he could puff up, Masters continued.

"I doubt that's the case but it does present another possibility, which, truthfully, I had not considered."

"Shall I call off the nine o'clock meeting, then?" Killroy

asked.

"No. I have the crime solved. I'm even quite sure what is in Adam's coded message but I just can't demonstrate it yet. There is still some time and the outcome of the several cases is not dependant upon it anyway."

"I'll see you at nine, then," Killroy said before turning to leave.

"Make it 8:45 right here, in case I need your assistance."

There was still the matter of Millie's whereabouts at the moment of the murder. As much as he disliked having to bring it up to her, he had put it off as long as he could.

Millie was making preparations for dinner. Masters took a seat and a cup of coffee.

"I'm fixing something we can eat quick this evening, there being the big meeting and all at nine," she announced.

"Smells wonderful whatever it is."

"Hungarian goulash. Another of my mama's recipes. She was a good cook. I've set up her French bread to rise, too. A Caesar salad, Hungarian goulash, and French Bread - quite a international spread, wouldn't you say, Mr. M?"

"Yes indeed."

Masters sat quietly for a moment gathering his thoughts and trying to formulate just the right words for his question.

"Something on your mind, big fella?" she asked.

"It shows, does it? Yes. There is. It has to do with exactly where you were at the time of Mr. Williams' murder."

"I figured we'd get around to that sooner or later. I've always been the World's worst liar. You probably know where I was. Raggs doesn't know how to tell a fib. I'm sure he saw me going into Guy's room."

"Well, actually, he says he didn't see you going in - just saw you heading in that direction with what looked to be a supply of linens."

"That's right, but I did take them inside."

"He keeps his door locked now."

"I'm the maid. I have keys. That's how it works when you're the maid."

"Yes, I suppose so."

"I said I was down here because I didn't want to be a suspect. For all the smiles and good humor you've seen from me, I've been scared outta my boots by this whole thing."

"Why is that?"

"I know I'm going to come into a lot of money from his Will. Mr. W. told me that himself a number of years ago. I figured that would be like a motive."

"Lots of folks seem to be in his will for large sums of money, Millie. Why would you think that you would be singled out as a suspect?"

"I've always been that way. Mama always seemed to know whenever I did something wrong. I'll admit I got into trouble more often than my sisters. I was just always at the wrong place at the wrong time. You can imagine in a house full of girls - if little sis could be blamed for their mischief, then let her take the punishment. I guess I still just expect to be blamed when things go wrong. That's mostly why I said what I said, I swear."

"Mostly?"

"Well, if you bought that I was down here then I couldn't say that I had seen Raggs in the hall outside the study. I figured whoever done it had to a been close by to the study and he and Guy was the only two others not inside the room. I didn't want to have to make him a suspect, you know?"

"I can understand that. So, you went on into Guy's room?"

"That's right. I laid two sheets and two pillowcases on his bed - that's how he has me do it. I tell him I'll be happy to make it up for him, but he always says he's perfectly able to do that himself."

"What was the position of the pull down stairs to the attic when you were in there?'

"I don't understand."

"In Guy's room, in the ceiling, there is a set of pull down stairs that lead up into the attic. Were they pulled down or were they folded up into the ceiling?"

"Up in the ceiling."

"Did you notice anything unusual about the couch?"

"Unusual? Well, his pillows always need fluffing, if that's what you mean. In fact, I was just on my way across the room to do that when I heard the commotion next door and ran out into the hall."

"The couch was right where it always is, then?"

"Hasn't moved from that spot in twenty years as far as I've seen. Guy is one who likes things to stay the same."

"And then you entered the study."

"Yes. I saw the light had fallen and poor Mr. Williams layin' there and I went right over to be with the girls."

"Do you suspect Raggs is involved in the murder?"

"Raggs. Hardly. He catches the spiders in this place and turns them loose in the park down the street. He ain't no killer."

"Okay then. Thank you."

"I'm sorry about lying to you, Mr. M. It's not really how I am."

"I'm sure that's true. Now, do I get a sneak preview of that goulash?"

"Sure, but you gotta come over here to the stove. I'm not about the drip it all over the floor."

* * * * * *

Killroy was entering Betty's office as Masters walked across the entry hall. He followed him inside.

"Mr. Madison, just the person I'm looking for. I have the prelims on the background check on Guy Lester. Did you know he used to be Guy Lassiter - same name as that Peter you figured did in Mr. Williams and the mailman."

Masters and Betty exchanged glances and the question was ignored. Masters took the report and scanned it hurriedly. "Seems to contain nothing really new. Apparently substantiates what both he and Dorothy have told us."

"Look at page seven, toward the bottom," Killroy insisted, surprising both Betty and Masters. "It says that right out of high school he worked for the Lombards - that's the Billy

Lombard gang that had the turf war with Adam Williams, Senior."

"I guess I didn't know about that," Masters said, looking at Betty for confirmation. She obliged.

"I just learned about it myself," Betty said and then continued. "The short of it is that old man Williams got squeezed out of the north and north east areas back into this western section. It had to do with booze and prostitution mostly. After that happened, it all settled down, I guess. When Senior died, and Adam took over, he got rid of the blatantly illegal activities and concentrated on making the fur business legit. He had a good head for business and was quite successful. I didn't know about Guy's involvement with Lombard."

Masters added a few things from what he had just read.

"From the report he seemed to have been an errand boy of some kind. Didn't last long, apparently. I suppose lots of young men got involved on the fringes of organized crime in those days – do anything for a dollar. Still, it may be worth pursuing. Also, it seems Guy had no alibi for the night of the liquor store robbery/murder. At first, when Jacks had been the only one who ID'ed Peter, the authorities thought it could have just as well been Guy, or Guy and Peter. Then, when the Larossa's came forward and verified Jacks' account, the investigation centered on Peter, and Guy was no longer a suspect."

Betty had some other news.

"The serial numbers from those hundred dollar bills Guy says he received in the mail on Monday came from the Lexington Avenue Bank - the same one Adam has always used. Interestingly, it is also the bank used by Alex, Millie, Guy and Raggs. So, I guess that's a dead end."

"Is it a large bank?"

"It has a dozen or so branches. The local branch is about two blocks from here - strictly walk in - no drive through. I once dated the head teller there. I'm not sure about its assets if that what you mean."

"Suppose you could ask a favor of that young man?"

"The Teller? Brad? Sure. We're good friends. What?"

"See if you can find out if anyone regularly withdraws five one hundred dollar bills on a weekly basis - probably on Friday, if I had to guess."

"Consider it done."

"If I'm right, ask the prettiest, single teller first. It should save time."

Betty gave him a look suggesting confusion. He did not explain further.

* * * * * *

Masters was back in his room. The phone rang. It had been an hour since speaking with Betty so he assumed it was she. It was.

"Right on all counts, Mr. M. The gorgeous teller with the low cut blouse says that every Friday noon Alex comes in and withdraws cash – twenty-five twenties and five hundreds."

"Good work, my dear."

The report prompted a short review and critique of what he knew and suspected.

Why would Alex be giving Guy five hundred dollars a week? If it were a payoff of some kind - blackmail, perhaps - why would Guy have even mentioned the money to me? Perhaps because he thought I would find out through some other means and he wanted to be covered ahead of time. If I saw regular deposits into his bank account above and beyond what his salary would allow, I might get suspicious. If it were a payoff for services rendered - like helping to murder Adam - the payments began well ahead of time. That would make sense, get the payment in advance or probably get nothing at all. Receive it in a series of small payments so there would be no suspicious trail. Those possibilities are intriguing.

Masters was ready for his presentation. He went over his notes one more time to make sure they would be presented in logical order. The moment of confronting the guilt party was always one of mixed emotions for Masters, particularly when he had grown fond of the perpetrator.

CHAPTER NINE:
Day three: Evening

The study was arranged essentially as it had been at the time of the murder. Five chairs had been added to accommodate the extra guests. The chandelier had been removed from the room and was replaced at the ceiling by a large, suspended, cardboard box. The room was lit by a dozen brass, scone wall lamps, with flame embossed, ornamental bulbs, which afforded a subdued, shadow laden aura to the scene.

By now the principal players are all familiar. Millie, Betty and Dorothy occupied the three seats on the west end of the gently curved seating arrangement. Alex and guy were on the East end. Next to them an Assistant States Attorney, Detective Killroy, and his Captain. John came in last and sat beside Killroy. Once they were all in place, Raggs took the remaining seat next to Dorothy. A uniformed policeman stood on each side of the door. Conversation had been left elsewhere. It was funeral quiet. Perhaps that was appropriate.

At exactly nine p.m. Masters came through the door and moved to a position behind the desk. He began speaking immediately.

"Last Monday morning Adam Williams strode to this position at exactly nine o'clock a.m. He sat in this chair as I am am doing now. He unlocked his middle desk drawer like this and removed a folder like this. He looked - briefly – at me, made a few terse remarks and then reached across the desk to hand me an envelope which contained a retainer check.

"Adam was a punctual man - everyone knew that. It was completely predictable that if the meeting had been scheduled for nine a.m. it *would* begin at precisely nine am. At 9:02 the chandelier dropped and Adam was killed. I scheduled this meeting for precisely nine o'clock this evening."

He looked at his watch.

"It is now 9:02"

In a sudden rush, the empty, cardboard box from the ceiling came crashing down, hitting Masters as he sat in the chair. Raggs and Killroy jumped to their feet. The women gasped. Alex sat unruffled and smiled, as if witnessing some center ring attraction at a tattered-tent traveling circus.

Masters brushed the box away and stood.

"You have just seen exactly how the deed was done. I will provide a complete explanation and demonstration of how the mechanism involved was able to do what you have witnessed - several of you twice, now. Please note that today, *all* of the suspects are right here in this room and you have my word that I did not use an accomplice.

"Let me begin by reviewing the important background information surrounding the murder of Adam Williams.

"By his own admission, he was not a likeable person. To investigate all those who had reason to dislike the man enough to kill him would take more days than I am likely to have left on this Earth. My investigation has therefore concentrated on those with the closest ties to this household – Dorothy, Alex, Guy, Millie, Raggs, Betty, and John Haven. Even among this small group, motives abound.

"As John suggested to me early on, he has one of the best motives – a ten million dollar life insurance policy. Further investigation suggests that, financially, he would have been far better off in the long run if the business remained as it was. He, of course, knew that better than anyone.

"Dorothy and Betty will both reportedly receive something in the neighborhood of thirty million each. That sum will surely quadruple for Dorothy once the business is sold. Alex's share is harder to estimate – properly handled it could perhaps reach over one hundred million over a period of several years. Guy, Millie and Raggs are each remembered in the Will with nearly a quarter of a million dollars each plus Raggs will go on drawing his paycheck until he dies.

"Alex has no need for the money. He earns a huge amount each year and his investments could support all of us here – in lavish style - for the rest of our years. Dorothy was assured of living in luxury forever just as things were and she detests taking care of investments and other business matters that will fall to her now that Adam is dead.

"Betty has modest tastes and was being well supported in her job. Ninety five percent of the money she will inherit was *not* included in the Will – a document, which Adam had her keep in her possession - but was set forth, instead, in a separate document about which she had no knowledge.

"So, for most of the possible suspects, money was a relatively mild motive. If, however, one were to approach the investigation as if it had been financially motivated, the suspects would seem to be narrowed down to the threesome of Guy, Millie and Raggs. There is a scenario that could make that work – Raggs with the engineering background, Guy with the mechanical hands and ready access to the attic, and Millie the final minute trigger person.

"Interestingly, that same threesome could be bonded through another motivation – finally being fed up with the shabby – often abusive – way in which Adam treated the two people they loved the most – Dorothy and Alex. Let me leave that for now and suggest other possibilities.

"Thirty-five plus years ago, Adam killed Raggs' father in a hit and run accident in London. He says that he harbors no ill will toward Adam, yet he is here and has arranged a lifetime income for himself whether Adam is alive or dead. He had the know-how to commit the crime and relatively easy access to the attic.

"Then we can't overlook the possible team of Dorothy and Alex. Perhaps they finally reached their limit with Adam. Alex is mechanically clever himself with just enough engineering background to understand the physical problem that would need to be solved. With them as the perpetrators the motive would necessarily be that of hate and revenge rather than greed.

"Guy, who quite clearly was Adam's prime suspect, has always loved Dorothy. He was terribly jealous of his brother during the time Peter seemed to be winning her heart. Although he might have had some chance to compete for her with Peter, he felt he had none against wealthy, charming, good looking, Adam. Enough motive for murder at this late date? Perhaps. Things can seethe inside for just so long.

There is a second possible picture involving Guy. The first coded message from Adam could be interpreted to mean that he was satisfied that it had been Guy who was responsible for Peter's murder. (Peter being the father reference and Alex being the nephew.) Since they were dead ringers for one another it could have been Guy and not Peter who pulled the robbery and killed the clerks and allowed Peter to take the blame. That would have given Guy a chance with Dorothy. The brothers had been known to fight each other viciously. Perhaps, when Adam approached Guy with the evidence, Guy decided to kill Adam so Dorothy would never know the truth. As I say – a marginal possibility.

"There is an outside player by the name of Johnny Lasrossa - the members of the household knew him as Johnny the Mailman. It is he who has cleared up much of the mystery in this case. He admits that he robbed Dorothy's safe of her jewels as at least partial payment for debts on which Adam had never made good. Johnny had been an errand boy for him many years ago. Adam decided the one way he could win Dorothy's hand in marriage was to have Peter killed while he was in prison. He had Johnny arrange for Peter's demise. He now tells us that it was Adam who paid him and his wife to bear false testimony against Peter at the trial and that it was Adam who set up the murders at the liquor store for the sole purpose of ridding himself of his competition for Dorothy.

"Why not just kill Peter and be done with it? The love triangle connection to Adam was too obvious. He would have surely been suspected. Johnny reported that rather than paying him as promised, Adam threatened to expose him as having lied at the trial - Adam having been careful to have sequestered Larossa and his wife with witnesses for six hour periods on both sides of the robbery. They would swear the two could not have been anywhere near the store at the time of the murders.

"*Perhaps* fifty thousand dollars worth of jewels - with a street value of ten or fifteen - was not enough revenge for Johnny and he arranged Adam's murder.

"Peter's two card playing friends had also been paid to occupy Peter that night and were then immediately provided work out of the area. With the Larossa's intimidated and Peter's alibis missing, it left only Jacks, who Adam dispatched from this Earth with a drunken stupor. Why kill him? Adam knew a wino could not be trusted past the promise of his next bottle. And what if Jacks had not died from the vodka? Larosssa was instructed to arrange a fall off a nearby building.

"Larossa fingered Ed Patchel as one of the three who Adam employed to pull the liquor store robbery. It was he who Adam paid to pull the trigger. Detective Killroy's ballistics lab has verified that the hand gun found in Adam's personal safe was the murder weapon in that crime. It bore Patchel's fingerprints. After the murder, Adam had Patchel return the weapon to him, ostensibly to destroy it so there would be no evidence against him. Once in hand, however, Adam turned the tables, as they say, and told Patchel if he ever revealed his connection with either Adam or the murders, Adam would see that the authorities received the weapon. This afternoon Ed Patchel was located and questioned and he confessed to the murders, essentially clearing the name of Peter Lassitor and effectively implicating Adam Williams."

Betty began weeping. Alex crossed his arms. Raggs

wore an expression of disbelief. Betty and Millie stared at each other.

"Had it, perhaps, been Mr. Patchel who had come back to take his own revenge against Adam? He certainly had a powerful motive. What we know for certain at this point is that Adam was responsible for the deaths of the two store clerks, Peter Lassiter and Mr. Jacks.

“Before I go further detailing motives and suspects I want to demonstrate just how Adam's murder was orchestrated. It was as ingenious a murder as I have ever investigated. Raggs, will you help me put our diorama up here on the desk?"

Masters arranged the phones out of the way close to the west end of the desk to make room and reached for the large calendar pad to remove it. Suddenly he stopped, picking up the calendar and scrutinizing it with narrowed eyes.

"If you will give me just a moment here, please,” he said slowly and deliberately.

He sat back down and removed the sheet containing the hyphen code from his pocket. Looking back and forth from it to the calendar he began marking the sheet. He motioned Betty and Killroy to come to his side and in hushed voices gave them instructions. They moved with the sheet and the calendar to the conference table in the rear.

Masters turned back to the gathered guests.

"Excuse that interruption but I believe I have just been able to decipher Adam's final code. Betty and the Detective will work it out and we will examine those findings later.

“Now, let's look at this model Raggs helped me build. The central room that you see here is this study - note the desk and the chandelier. The room to your left is Guy's quarters which provides access to the attic over the study. The room to your right is Alex's studio. The two sides of the attic are seen on top separated by this rock fire wall.

"In the attic above the study we found a pull wire - a triggering mechanism of sorts that fed through a pipe in the rear wall and to a handle outside of Guy's window. The inside end was attached to a stick of wood. It was made to appear that that stick had been run through the holes in the metal collar and the matching holes in the top of the chandelier – replacing the metal rod - and that at the time of the murder the handle was tugged, pulling the stick out of the holes allowing the chandelier to fall. That mechanism could not have worked for several reasons - the stick was not strong enough to support the weight; that weight, even had the stick been strong enough, would have pressed so hard onto the stick that no one could have slid it out of the holes by pulling on the wire; and the acute angle between the stick and the rear wall would have made it impossible for the stick to have been pulled loose.

"The device was clearly provided as a false lead to temporarily cast suspicion somewhere other than where it belonged - unless *that* was the intention - to make it appear clearly false and lead us away from Guy, the obvious target of the devise. It not being the trigger, we were forced to look search further.

"Now, note this table in the studio - it is Alex's clay table. Note the string that I have strung from the top of the chandelier in the attic, east, hidden under the insulation to the firewall and through it - there was a second pipe in place just below the insulation. The string then crosses several yards of the attic floor above the studio and is directed down into the studio through still another brass pipe, this one curved to ease the friction of the 90 degree angle through the ceiling.

"Let me back up for a moment to the collar into which the chandelier was secured and the modifications made by the perpetrator. First, the chandelier was supported in place with a rope tied to the short crossbeam directly above the hole. Recent rope fibers suggest that is true. The metal support rod was then removed. The stick from the false lead was indeed inserted into the *west* hole, but just a half inch or so – just far enough to support a small portion of the weight. Into the hole on the other side was inserted a well lubricated, metal rod about five inches long - plenty strong enough to support the entire weight so the stick merely had to help keep the chandelier straight up and down in the collar. The supporting rope was then removed. In the other end of the small metal rod was a hole through which a string was strung – not tied."

Masters pointed to the string he had spoken of earlier and traced its course from the little rod, under the insulation through the pipe in the wall, across the attic floor to the curved pipe and down through the ceiling of the studio. The other end also went from the little rod, back through the pipe, but it was secured on the other side of the wall to a nail in the floor of the attic just above the studio.

"Even with the rod so well lubricated, it would take a substantial force to move it the half inch necessary to release the chandelier. The power for that was provided on the clay table, directly below the hole in the ceiling. Someone with very good mechanical savvy, ready access to the studio, and knowledge of Alex's new, oversized alarm clock then rigged an ingenious power boosting gadget using the gear box from a toy truck - also generally known to be available in the studio.

"Through the gear box, enough mechanical advantage was produced so that when the alarm went off, unwinding the spring and turning the winding lever in reverse on the back of the clock, the string would be wound onto a small, wooden, attached wheel, pulling the pin in the attic. With the support of the steel rod gone, the wooden stick splintered under the weight and immediately gave way, falling down onto the attic floor near the metal collar. As I indicated, the string, rather than being tied in a knot at the hole in the small rod, had been threaded through that hole and strung back through the pipe in the firewall and secured to a nail on the floor in the attic above the studio. In that way when the clock wound the longer end of the string, it eventually drew the little rod tight against the pipe in the wall - the hole in the pipe was too small to accept the 3/4 inch rod. Later the perpetrator untied the string from the nail and pulled it loose through the eye in the rod, leaving the rod under six inches of insulation on the other side – the study side - of the fire wall, with no incriminating string attached to it.

"I noticed a small discoloration on the ceiling above the clay table. It was similar to one Millie had pointed out in her kitchen. The spot had been maintained for years because the hole had been patched with a different variety of plaster from the original. Close examination of the spot on the ceiling revealed it was directly under a hole in the attic floor above. When the material used to fill the hole in the ceiling plaster was analyzed today it was found to be plaster of Paris - easily available in the studio. More helpful still, it held the fingerprint of the person who patched the hole.

"The alarm was set to go off at 9:02. The perpetrator was therefore able to be elsewhere, legitimately alibied by others at the moment the chandelier fell and killed Adam Williams. The triggering mechanism – the short rod - had been pulled away and hidden in the insulation. I'm sure the murderer planned to recover it when the opportunity arose. It didn't arise soon enough and we located it first.

The would-be killer was patient, waiting for the right opportunity. The time for the murder had been set, unknowingly, by Adam himself. The gathering presented a setting that was perfect in every way - I'm sure far beyond the killer's fondest dreams. The irony, no doubt, provided additional satisfaction – pleasure even - for the perpetrator.

"Of all the players, only one harbored the necessary combination of hatred, revenge, and know-how. At the time of the jewel robbery, someone was inquisitive enough to examine the remaining contents of Dorothy's safe. He or she went snooping, leaving fingerprints on virtually every paper and cellophane window on the envelopes in her safe. It was there the person discovered documents that indicated Alex was not Adam's son but Peter's. It was there that person made the connection between Peter and Guy - that they were brothers. It was there the person saw prom pictures of Dorothy and Peter and pictures of Peter in the clippings about the murder trial.

"That person then researched Peter's trial and ferreted out the same incriminating information that my investigation eventually discovered - that Adam had in fact had Peter framed for murder and then, uneasy about the wheels of justice, had him killed in prison. It is the same person whose fingerprint was found in the plaster of Paris patch on the ceiling of the studio.

The case was cinched by several things: that fingerprint, that same print on the burned out Edison bulb from the attic, the insulation that had clung to the fishing line used as the string – strong line that I was given, by the way - and bits of insulation Millie removed from the killer's sweater later on the morning of the murder – insulation which had rubbed off the fishing line as it was being rewound onto the reel after having served its murderous purpose.

"Lilly's fingerprints on the new bulb in the attic were a fluke – she had apparently handled the bulb while in the studio and that bulb had been taken to replace the one in the attic – perhaps or perhaps not to implicate Alex.

"I must admit the first thing that turned me in the right direction in this case was wondering why one would need to be able to see the face of an alarm clock clear across a room when the sole purpose of having it was to sound an alarm so you didn't have to keep watching it! There had to be some other reason for a mechanical – wind up – clock, and the most logical other reason would somehow be related the very powerful, long lasting spring drive it possessed."

"And, finally, there was the matter of the signature on the death threats. It appears that Adam missed the ultimate taunt intended by those threats. The signature echoed the *one and only* perverted time Adam seemed pleased with Alex and had called him his little man – an event so powerful that Alex seems to have been trying to relive it over and over again only to then vent his hatred of the man onto his female companions once the comfort has passed."

Alex began clapping slowly and stood up.

"I knew you were good, Masters, but I had no idea how good. I admit it. Everyone in this room must know in his heart that I did the World a great favor by killing Adam Williams. It wasn't all just for my own selfish pleasure. The World needed to be rid of him. I don't apologize although I am sorry for you, dear Mom, and you, sweet Millie."

With a nod from the States Attorney, relayed by the Captain to his men, the uniformed policeman escorted Alex from the room.

Masters addressed Guy directly.

"The money you began receiving was from Alex, a way of thanking you, I suppose, once he discovered from the contents of Dorothy's safe that you were his uncle. He knew that the wire and handle apparatus would never convict you but hoped it would confuse things long enough for him to retrieve the actual triggering rod. He may have also hoped that our investigation of your background would unearth the connection between Adam and Peter's murder."

Masters turned back to the group as a whole.

"And why through cryptograms: I can only imagine that Alex found some twisted irony in using one of Adam's passions as the means to make him squirm one final time."

Killroy approached Masters with the sheet he and Betty had been working on.

Masters explained: "The hyphen code was based on calendar dates, used in a special manner as abstrusely implied by Adam at the outset of the code. The number to the left of each hyphen represented the month of the year - January by one, December by twelve, and so on. The 0-0 did indeed represent W and had to be added since there are no W's in the spelling of any of the months. The number *after* the hyphen is the letter within that month. *One Hyphen One* would take you to January - the first month - and 'J' - the first letter in January. 4-4 would be the fourth letter in the fourth month - April or 'I'. In this way the letter 'A' could be represented in several ways: 1-2, 1-5, 2-6, 8-1 and so on. Because of those many options for most of the letters, a one for one, cryptogram-like, substitution could not be made between the code and the alphabet during decoding. It was a twelve-base system - the twelve months - once the 0-0 was discounted as making it falsely appear to be a thirteen-base system.

"It is my Hunch that the hyphen-coded message contains Adam's confession relating to the murder of Peter and that is why he concealed it so well in the code he chose. Why would he confess at all? Probably to serve his huge ego even after death. Laughing at us for having been so inept as to not have discovered his secret. As I said, that is my hunch. Detective Killroy, will you read the actual message as you and Betty have just decoded it."

Killroy stood - proudly at attention - to the west of the desk. He cleared his throat and began reading:

"I HAVE BEEN A DESPICABLE HUMAN BEING. I DIDN'T LEARN HOW TO BE OTHERWISE, NOR DID I TRY. I WANTED DOROTHY MORE BECAUSE I COULDN'T WIN HER HEART THAN BECAUSE I LOVED HER. LOVE AND I ARE STRANGERS. WINNING AND I ARE LOVERS. SO, I FRAMED HER BELOVED PETER, PAYING WITNESSES AND PERPETRATORS AND CONSUMING FOUR INNOCENT LIVES IN THE PROCESS. THE RECORD SHOULD BE SET STRAIGHT. IT'S ALRIGHT TO DO THAT NOW BECAUSE WITHOUT <u>THIS</u> DOCUMENT I HAD COMMITTED THE PERFECT CRIME.

ADAM PAUL WILLIAMS"

Killroy addressed his final, surprisingly astute, comment to the portrait of Adam which stared lifelessly from behind the desk.

"I'm afraid it was *not* the perfect crime, Mr. Williams. It seems that both Alex *and* <u>you</u> misjudged the skill that your chosen investigator, Raymond Masters, would bring to bear on *The Case of the Cryptogram Murders."*

THE END

Other Books from *THE FAMILY OF MAN PRESS*

www.familypress.com

More Mystery/Suspense Novels
(Adult and young adult)

The Murder No One Committed: A Raymond Masters Mystery - Garrison Flint

While consulting with a noted writer as she prepares her newest book, Raymond Masters, a retired criminal investigator is confronted with her murder. The writer had been openly hated by those who worked for her and each suspect harbors more than enough motive to want her dead. The more clues he uncovers, the more obvious becomes his conclusion: "This is a murder no one committed." (He solves it, of course! Can you beat him to discovering the unusual twist this case presents?)

The Case of the Smiling Corpse: A Raymond Masters Mystery - Garrison Flint

Masters is asked to assist the home town police solve the murder of a retired banker. Was it the teen age boy whose car had killed the banker's wife; the waitress at the local café with a special interest in the handyman who, it turns out, is handy with things others than tools; the sister-in-law who may inherit the victim's estate; or a hit man hired by his wife before she was killed? Initially, it looks like suicide as the body is found in a room locked from the inside with a pistol beside the body. Perhaps it was the perfect (almost) frame. The reader will have to wait until the final paragraph to hear the old inspector's solution.

A Gathering of Killers: A Raymond Masters Mystery - Garrison Flint

Inspector Masters is at it again - this time untangling the mystery of a murder in which the body was stabbed, shot, strangled, drowned, poisoned and bludgeoned. A dozen suspects at the beautiful Whispering Pines Lodge lead him on a merry chase as he systematically sorts away the innocent and hones in on the culprit (or is it culprits?). Again, it remains until the final page to hear the old inspector's solution.

The Man Who Refused to Die: A Raymond Masters Mystery - Garrison Flint

Not even the third time was to be the charm for this murderer. A beloved, retired, dying, classical guitarist is the eventual victim. In his mansion - curiously - live his three former wives, his long time back-up guitarist with his despicable son, his distant personal assistant, the charming young chauffeur with a shady past, the cook and the mysterious stranger. There is a twist at the end unlike the readers of Raymond Masters mysteries have ever before witnessed.

Revenge of the Restless Crossbow: A Raymond Masters Mystery - Garrison Flint

Apparently of its own volition, an antique crossbow, long perched high up on the wall of the Rafferty Mansion, fires and kills one of the guests at a publisher's book launching party. The following day another member of the group is found murdered. There are a variety of suspects: three mystery writers, a universally disliked book critic, the cantankerous neighbor and his son, the wily old grounds keeper, the maid, the new assistant to Winston Rafferty (one of the writers), and a flock of pigeons. Nothing is simple this time out. The twists and turns tangle among themselves. Masters identifies the perpetrator, of course, but the reader will have to wait until the final word of the final paragraph to hear his/her name.

The Case of the Gypsy Curse: A Raymond Masters Mystery - Garrison Flint

Seven of the past nine leaders of an off-beat fraternal order in a small Wyoming town died mysterious deaths. There have been no wounds and no traces of poison. There has, however, been a long-standing Gypsy curse against the group. Natural causes? Coincidence? Curse? Masters doesn't think so. Not only, does he nail the perpetrator(s?) of these seven crimes, but he puts the screws to four more along the way.

The Case of the Clairvoyant Kid: A Raymond Masters Mystery
Garrison Flint

At age 15 handsome, Hans Hanzik – a Bosnian orphan – is the most successful touring psychic in the U.S. A series of threats against his life brings Detective Masters into the case. Masters immediately senses trouble (the boy's guardian) and conj ours up a spell or two of his own. Though set in the Ozark Mountains, Masters manages to solve 3 outstanding homicides form NYC and Key West, while tutoring the shy, sheltered young clairvoyant in the gentle art of romance. In a spine tingling finish, Masters saves the boy and zaps the bad guys.

The Case of the Cryptogram Murders: A Raymond Masters Mystery – Garrison Flint

Adam Williams, wealthy furrier and despicable human being, is killed while Detective Masters and the half dozen possible suspects from family and staff are with him in his study - each the perfect alibi for the others. Motives and gadgetry abound. Along the way four other murders are solved as Masters enlists the help of a fascinating group of characters - all of them suspects.

The Murders at Terrapin Island: A Raymond Masters Mystery- Garrison Flint

The late July vacation, which Raymond Masters had been looking forward to at the *Terrapin Island* resort in Lake Huron, immediately turns to work as staff members, one after another, are murdered. Could it be the troubled teenage boy, the greedy millionaire or his pants chasing wife, the impatient artist, or the beautiful young writer who claims she is searching for her birth mother? Other suspects abound as Masters sorts through the clues with the reader.

The Butler Did It! A Raymond Masters Mystery - Garrison Flint

Detective Raymond Masters arrives at *Windstone Manor* - high atop a tiny, remote, snow blown, island off the Maine Coast - to supervise a Scavenger Hunt designed by Elliott Stone, the aging, despicable, Lord of the Manor, to allow one of his heirs to enhance his or her position in his will. The participants include the five butlers who formerly worked for him (most of whom hate each other and Elliott), his brother and sister (who harbor long standing grudges against him), and his nephew (a self-centered, amoral, 30 year old who has lived most of his life at Windstone). Then there is Carl, his lawyer; Bea, his nurse and secretary; Angie, the cook and maid; and Hyde, the current young butler. Five bodies later, Masters (once again surviving a strange little policeman sidekick) solves the cases amid the unrelenting, freezing storm that holds the group captive on the island.

The Case of the Despicable Duo: A Raymond Masters Mystery Garrison Flint

No one shed a tear when either of them (a wealthy father and his adult son) were murdered but when one of Raymond Masters' friends is accused of doing them in, the old detective packs his bags and arrives to direct the investigation. In this twelfth book in the series, legitimately motivated suspects abound, including the maid, long mistreated by both men; the handyman, a loner and newcomer to the area; the brother, an expert marksman who had a life long feud with the family; the security guard, with unspoken motives; the drifter, whose presence seems oddly out of place; the brilliant teenage twins next door, with tempers and revenge on their minds; and their mother, recently done wrong by the son. The shot had clearly come from his friend's bedroom window yet Masters works to prove otherwise.

The Case of the Murders at Fairfield Heights: A Raymond Mastery Mystery by Garrison Flint

Fairfield Heights, a century old mansion, offers a haunting presence as it sits high atop a dreary, rock strewn, hill. The ailing, ninety-two year old billionaire, Jasper Fairfield, gathers his heirs for the disbursement of his fortune. One by one they are murdered. Is it the help, hoping to maintain their hold on the property? Is it one of the sons - Farley, certifiably deranged, or Chester, the seldom serious laugh machine? Or, how about the two adult grandchildren - Bernice, single, educated, selfish; and Cliff, the one truly sane appearing individual in the lot. Maybe it is Cliff's fifteen year old son, who quietly seethes underneath his affable demeanor. The case presents one unusual twist for the old detective: He sees the victims alive and well *after* the time of death certified by the coroner!

Red Grass at Twilight: A suspense mystery -
Garrison Flint

A bright, mild-mannered, middle aged man struggles to regain his memory while being forced to evade ugly adversaries who seem determined to stop him before that can occur. Why are so many people pursuing him? He is not at all certain which side of the law his antagonists are on and that leaves his own position in doubt - good guy or bad guy? Because of that uncertainty, he can't engage the help of the police. From the opening page in which he "emerges from a dark cloud of nothingness" possessing only two bags and an all-encompassing sense of foreboding, to the final, nail-biting, terrifying scene high atop a hotel roof, the reader is kept guessing.

Other Ozark Ghost Stories by *Marc Miller*

The Specters of Carlton County
Marc Miller, *Ghost writer*

To this day the ghosts of six, teenage, confederate soldiers - *The Cowards' Patrol* - roam the Ozark backwoods, forced by an evil cleric to continue taking the war to blue clad Yankees who dare trespass into the dark summer nights of isolated, Carlton County. When a young writer, Marc Miller, travels to the area to write their story, he finds he is unwelcome both as a writer and an outsider. He hears their mournful cries at night and sees their ghostly images in the windows and mirrors of the old Inn. He encounters them on horseback, swords at the ready, galloping together across a foggy, moonlit, Civil War graveyard. Are they apparitions searching for their final peace, or are they something more sinister? Miller is a skeptic but will that continue once he meets *The Specters of Carlton County*?

The Malevolent Ghost of Charlie Chance:
Marc Miller. *Ghost Writer*

The Ozark Hills Academy - a rustic boarding school - sits atop a beautiful hill in the back country of Northwest Arkansas, and serves the region's disadvantaged, 13 to 19 year old boys. The area had once been owned by the long dead, Charlie Chance - known hater of children and progress. During each *Devil's Darkness* - the convergence of the dark of the moon and a strong, warm, southerly breeze - the Ghost of old Charlie selects a student and sucks his soul from his being, leaving him dead and bereft of an afterlife. Author, Marc Miller, hoping to write Charlie's story, arrives to investigate. The Ghost appears and raises havoc in an apparent attempt to get the writer to leave. It becomes a 'good ghost' - 'bad ghost' quandary for Marc and the young people who offer help.

The Kettles and the Keeps: Ghosts at War – An Ozark Mt. Ghost Story
Marc Miller, Ghost Writer

Ghost Writer, Marc Miller, arrives in *Sandy Valley*, an isolated area of northwest Arkansas, to mediate a dispute between warring clans of ghosts - the Kettles and the Keeps who, in their mortal forms, have been feuding for more than a century. A pair of pre-Civil War Apparitions appears - one Kettle and one Keep - and unexplainably begins inflicting serious physical maladies on a dozen teenagers. The dispute escalates, once again turning the families against each other. Marc enlists the help of Willy, a teenager suddenly confined to a wheelchair and Jake, a ten year old, wise beyond his years.

The Haunting of Hickory Hollow
Marc Miller, Ghost Writer

The tiny, backwoods, town of Hickory Hollow is haunted. It has been since before the Civil War. That ís just they way its residents want it. They have configured a mini-theme park around the ghostly goings on and seem to have established an amicable relationship with them. Marc Miller is brought into town when mysterious accidents - some resulting in the death of local residents - begin taking place. Is it the ghostly revenge predicted by the lore? Is it the more a worldly activity related to a business takeover? There are teenage ghosts swinging from ropes, bands of galloping ghostly desperados, and suspicious strangers. And then there is the secret *Covenant* sworn to by the locals residents. Hmmm!

Printed in the United States
214626BV00001B/67/A

9 781885 631695